WALTON WELL

CULTURE ART POETRY FICTION SOCIAL JUSTICE

PRESS

ALSO BY CHUCK ROSENTHAL

NOVELS

Loop's Progress
Experiments with Life and Deaf
Loop's End
Elena of the Stars
Avatar Angel, the Last Novel of Jack Kerouac
My Mistress Humanity
The Heart of Mars
Coyote O'Donohughe's History of Texas
Ten Thousand Heavens
The Legend of La Diosa
You Can Fly
The Hammer, the Sickle and the Heart
Let's Face the Music and Dance

MEMOIR

Never Let Me Go

ESSAYS

Are We Not There Yet? Travels in Nepal, North India, and Bhutan
West of Eden: A Life in 21st Century Los Angeles
How the Animals Around You Think: The Semiotics of Animal Cognition

POETRY (WITH GAIL WRONSKY)

Tomorrow You'll Be One of Us
The Shortest Farewells Are the Best

AWAKE FOR EVER IN A SWEET UNREST

Chuck Rosenthal

WALTON WELL PRESS
Los Angeles   Oxford

Editor: Theresia de Vroom
Contributing Editor: Jane Crawford
Intern Readers: Eve Harrison & Connor Wilson

Cover Design & Typesetting: ash good

Published by Walton Well Press
Los Angeles | Oxford

Hardcover ISBN: 978-1-964295-00-8
Paperback ISBN: 978-1-964295-01-5

Library of Congress Control Number: 2024908399

WALTONWELLPRESS.COM

For the Poets

Foreword

Was it a vision, or a waking dream?
Fled is that music:——Do I wake or sleep?

JOHN KEATS, "ODE TO A NIGHTINGALE"

"You must read Dante," he said to her. "If you are Beatrice. Beatrice is love, suspended by the thread of time between two eternities."

Is that what she had done? Fallen between eternities? She stood before him. "You don't really remember me," she said.

EXCHANGE BETWEEN KEATS AND BEATRIZ,
CHUCK ROSENTHAL, *AWAKE FOR EVER IN A SWEET UNREST*

The cover of this book features the 1870 painting by the Pre-Raphaelite painter, Dante Gabriel Rossetti. It depicts his beloved muse and deceased wife, Elizabeth Siddal (d. 1862). It is a painting that was done in several versions, inspired by Dante Alighieri's own muse, Beatrice Portanari, who was first memorialized at the moment of her death in his prose/poem of 1294, "La Vita Nuova," a work the painter, Dante Rossetti himself, translated.[1] Dante Alighieri's Beatrice, despite her pre-mature earthly demise, would live on long after her death to inspire his greatest work, the tri-part "Comedia," an account of many things, including the state of souls after death.

In the painting we see the ecstatic, dying, wife, model, and muse. Behind her stands the figure of the poet, Dante, on her left, and the figure of Eros, or love, on her right. A depiction of the love that inspires art and poetry? Perhaps. Beatrix looks toward heaven with her eyes closed, while a bird, the messenger

---

[1] *La Vita Nuova* had been a story that Rossetti had found of interest from childhood, and he had begun work translating it into English in 1845 and published it in his work *The Early Italian Poets*.

of death, drops a poppy into her hands, symbolic of the laudanum, the opiate to which she was addicted, and which would be the ultimate cause of her death.[2] A sundial, an ancient clock of sorts and a reminder that the time has come, sits behind her; the city of Florence and its landmark bridge, the "Ponte Vecchio," frame this enigmatic depiction.

Rosetti's painting is called "Beata Beatrix," (or "Beautiful Beatrix") an echo of Chuck Rosenthal's "Beatriz," and Dante's own "Beatrice."

In his novel Chuck Rosenthal, like Rosetti and Dante, before him investigates the place where inspiration, beauty, love, poetry, nature and mortality intersect. In his case it is not a city or a bridge, or the inspiration of a great poet, or the promise of everlasting life that connects them, but rather a secret library which traduces time and mortality, refurbished in the hands of a nineteen-year-old "reader" of sorts. It is her experience of meeting the poets themselves in a modern version of a medieval dream vision that Rosenthal so vividly and yet enigmatically investigates.[3]

The nineteenth century saw an explosion in music, art, fiction and poetry known as the "romantic movement" or "romanticism" which was characterized by a variety of elements that became the watershed, depicted in Rosenthal's novel, for all poetry and fiction to come afterward: these romantics are the basis of his library in the book, a library that ironically is situated in the basement of a bookstore, propping up the books that followed it. The Romantic movement was characterized in part by a devotion to and worship of nature and beauty; the solitary life and individualism vs. "in society;" a belief in the imagination—the "lamp" which illuminates while casting shadows vs. the "mirror" which mimetically reflects; an interest in the Gothic and the unknown; the ghost story, the legend or the folk tale; or as Rosenthal's Byron tells Beatriz, a preference for "...magic to knowledge," the super-natural , the weird or uncanny. Romanticism explores the revival of medieval tales such as those associated with the King Arthur myths; personal exploration and the creation of the romantic hero; the re-instatement of the muse or inspiration more generally, and the removal of boundaries. At the same time a unique group of artists, the Pre-Raphaelites, developed on a parallel course of which Rossetti was a front runner.

---

[2] In an 1873 letter to his friend and Pre-Raphaelite British textile designer, William Morris, Rossetti was adamant that it does not represent Siddal's death rather it portrays her as in a trance or an altered spiritual state.

[3] Dante's "Vita Nuova," in the mode of Boethius' "Consolation of Philosophy," like Rosenthal's novel, might be best described as a dream vision—which in Rosenthal's version of the popular genre is renewed and remastered.

But what these poets and writers have in common, like Dante, was their search for a new language. In Dante's case (as in Chaucer's) it was to write in the vernacular—Italian, (or English, in Chaucer's case) which everyone spoke—as opposed to Latin, which was reserved for the clergy, the elite, and the educated. The Pre-Raphaelites sought to literally paint in the style before Raphael, containing a purer and more natural light, an attention to nature and detail, far away from the mannerist leanings post-Raphael. So too the British Romantics sought out the language of the "common man," even if they sometimes strayed far afield. The rather unschooled Beatriz of Rosenthal's imagination, nonetheless, is their perfect "tabula rasa." And in Rosenthal's palimpsest, where time intercepts writing, she is the perfect subject to understand what it really means to read, which is to lose oneself in time and space entirely.

Following the watershed of the "Lyrical Ballads" (1798) by Wordsworth and Coleridge, Rosenthal's subjects are Keats, Shelley, Coleridge, and Byron, who are guided to our heroine, Beatriz, by the novelist Mary Shelley, in a real or imagined journey into the past. There, this "ghost from the future," Beatriz, meets them. And like the very act of reading itself falls into their history and into an impossible if plausible conundrum, or as Rosenthal (via Keats) sums it up: "You can't travel in time," Keats said to her. "We travel inside what we are, what we were. No more." But of course, we can travel in time, according to Rosenthal's novel if we discover or uncover the past by reading it and thus re-enacting it as if had not yet happened.

And this finally brings us to the question summed up by Dante Alighieri, Dante Gabriel Rossetti, and Chuck Rosenthal which is who is really the creative force in a work of art? Is it the artist—poet or writer in this case—or is it the reader? Dante stands behind Rosetti's fictional Beatrix in his painting just as the historical Dante Alighieri stands at a very far distance from his Beatrice, whom he only met twice in his youth.[4] Have they created her, or has she created them? If Beatriz is their reader (and in her act of cataloguing them, their historian and thereby the potential preserver of their library) is she not also their witness, their retelling, their immortality, keeping them as well as herself in Rosenthal's account, "Awake For Ever in a Sweet Unrest"? In the end in the book's final pages, perhaps it is ironically only the monster, the creation of Dr. Frankenstein and a fictional character, with Beatriz in tow, who know the answer to the question Rosenthal brilliantly poses.

—Theresia de Vroom, *Editor*

---

[4] Under circumstances which were hardly ideal or conclusive given the extent of her influence over one of the world's greatest poets.

Acknowledgements

This novel implicitly relies on the original work of John Keats, Mary Shelley, Percy Bysshe Shelley, Lord Byron, Samuel Taylor Coleridge and William Hazlitt. I also source a number of crisscrossing biographies of each of them, as well as of Leigh Hunt, Edward Trelawny, William Godwin, and William Wordsworth. Of course, *Awake* is a novel, without unnecessary commitment to chronology, fact, actual events, or biographies. My interests revolve around who these people were *as characters*, how they would act and what they would say when placed in the circumstances that unfold as the story develops.

I'd like to give special thanks to my publisher and chief editor at Walton Well Press, Theresia de Vroom, without whose enthusiasm, encouragement and intelligence this book would not exist. I'd also like to thank Jane Crawford for her meticulous and gentle advice concerning my syntactical idiosyncrasies. Special thanks to Catherine Segurson and Elizabeth McKenzie for publishing the opening chapters in *Catamaran*. Thank you, Elizabeth, for your friendship and your critical support over the years. Thank you, David St. John, for your inspiration and poetry. Thanks to Michael Ventura and Jazmin Aminian Ventura, for your enthusiastic support and critical reading. Thanks, Robert Eversz, for your detective eyes of the imagination. Thanks, Molly Bendall and Daniel Tiffany, for your herds of ideas. And thank you Alicia Partnoy and Antonio Leiva for guiding me to the tiny grocery in the village of Praiano on the cliffs of southern Italy, and much more. Thank you, ash good, amazing book designer, for your brilliant work on this book.

As always, my thanks to Gail Wronsky who taught me Surrealism and poetry, and during long gorgeous nights helped engineer, in process, the structure of this narrative.

My thanks to Beyond Baroque, the present tense setting of this novel, and to the poets there who for decades have filled me with metaphor and meaning deeper than meaning. —C.R.

AWAKE FOR EVER IN A SWEET UNREST

I

She parked in front of the building. Late evening, there was yet no one there. Beyond Baroque, once the city hall of Venice, California, though Venice was no longer a city. A citadel of poetry, of poets, when you entered you became one without choosing, though here, outside its doors, on Venice Blvd, there wasn't even a parking meter because who would park in front of poetry?

She wasn't as old as the century, only nineteen. Sometimes she worked in the bookstore, to the left of the entryway, a volunteer, unpaid, but that earned her a key to the front door, the bookstore, the theater, the art gallery upstairs, and to the latest haunting oddity, a catacomb discovered when the staff and arts board raised enough donations to build an extension in the garden at the back.

A stairway descended to a door that opened to a dark maze of books, thousands and thousands of books, some as old as the 19th century. There were no electrical outlets, no electric lighting. As Beatriz found when she entered, neither was there cell phone reception and, mysteriously, her laptop didn't function. The director of the Beyond Baroque bookstore, Christina Acevedo, apparently knew all this, but now, what could be done? The logistics of refurbishing the library catacomb, including the finances, were insurmountable; the decision to remove the books or blindly destroy them, for an institution dedicated to the preservation of literature, reprehensible.

Acevedo was short with a cascade of wavy, black hair. She occupied a small office at the back of the bookstore. Now sixty, she'd worked as an art museum administrator in San Francisco, later as an adjunct poetry writing instructor at UCLA. Widowed, here at Beyond Baroque she now worked for peanuts. On her book-lined wall, amidst hundreds of poetry books, were a handful of her own.

Beatriz pointed to them when they first met. "You write poetry," Beatriz said.

Christina Acevedo took off her glasses, squinted, then put them back on. She looked Beatriz in the eyes and said, "Who doesn't?"

Beatriz, though quite literate, was a high school dropout. Her parents were retired literature professors. They had pensions and books. Beatriz moved back in with them during the pandemic and didn't go back to school. She lived in a one room cottage studio in the backyard, lived on a small allowance, and drove an old Nissan.

Beyond Baroque stood near a city fire station and just then sirens broke out with their supernatural red wail that somehow made you feel closer to God, or hell. The two women stood silently as the engines and sirens roared past. When the outdoor noise was reduced to street traffic Christina straightened her glasses. Beatriz wore jeans, sneakers, and a white blouse. In a slow, gentle gesture Christina stepped toward her and dusted some cobwebs from her shoulders.

"You've been in the haunted cellar?" Christina said.

Beatriz loosened her tawny hair and let it fall to her shoulders. "No, just outside. But there's nothing in there but dark and books," she said.

"Worlds," said Christina.

"No lights?"

"You'll have to bring your own light, mi hija," Christina said. "Do you want a job?"

"Paying?" said Beatriz.

"In satisfaction and solitude." The bookstore would provide a flashlight and lantern, pencils, and paper. "Someone needs to record what's down there."

She needed to think. In her cottage that night she read Flaubert's "A Simple Heart." Emily Brontë's *Wuthering Heights* lay at her feet. Slowly, she sipped a can of beer and a shot of rye whisky. She had no television, but she could find whatever she wanted on her cell, though she didn't want any of that. She wanted wilder and deeper, and there was never anything wild or deep on video screens. She thought of the vast book cellar and her conversation with Christina. She hadn't worked for the bookstore long, nor spent much time with Acevedo. She'd only shelved and organized obscure books by obscure authors. But if there was something decisive in Acevedo's brown, sparkling eyes, there was yet something evasive, something leading or bleeding, something held back, some unnamed desire to share a secret. Worlds, she'd said, yet all books held worlds, all things did, every egg, every flower, every blade of grass; isn't that what the poets said, and now the philosophers and scientists too, but so what? what did that change? but for one moment in the mind of one person, a miracle was imagined, while meanwhile the sky fell, the forests burned, diseases spawned, in the streets people shot each other down.

She looked across the yard to her parents' house. A dim light glowed from a window where her father and mother undoubtedly sat across from each other on either side of two black candles, listening to someone on the flute, Eric Dolphy perhaps, remembering the dead and how they died. There was no permanence to love, it didn't solve being alone or waiting to be alone. She wondered what reached across one generation to the next besides death. Is this why she might spend her days, her time, in a tomb of books? Let us go there, you and I . . . who was you, who was I?

She spent the next day watching the October sun lower itself across the southern sky until it touched the ocean; had some soup and a glass of red wine, then drove to Beyond Baroque. She didn't know why she expected Christina Acevedo there, at this evening hour, but she did and she was right. The doors to the building were locked and she let herself in, then unlocked the bookstore. Christina sat at her desk lit by a single small lamp.

"You're here," said Beatriz.

Christina blinked, took and let out a deep breath. "I can be alone anywhere," she said. "But I seldom succeed. Like now."

"I'm sorry," said Beatriz.

Christina pointed to a nearby bookshelf where, in front of a row of small press novels sat a lantern, a flashlight, a yellow legal pad, a pencil, and a box of matches.

"Light the lantern before you go in. The flashlight will stop working. Nothing works down there."

"You've been in," Beatriz said.

"Of course. But it's not really a place where you can spend much time."

"Sounds like the place for me," said Beatriz.

Christina laughed a little and then Beatriz did, too.

"Has anyone else tried to do this?" Beatriz asked.

"Lee, the boy before you, but let's save the stories. I'll keep kerosene for you in the first restroom."

Beatriz took the lantern up the broad stairs to the first restroom, the old men's room, though it was multi-gender now, the men's-women's room thing long gone, though during her brief time here she used the old women's room, simply from habit. The men's restroom hadn't been altered in years. Across from the stalls, five tall porcelain urinals stood vertically against the wall, an odd sight; they had to be older than her, much older, a chrome flush handle atop each one. She flushed one. The water poured down; the toilet swished. The kerosene sat on the windowsill at the back of the room, overlooking the back garden that hid the book tomb. She filled her lantern and contemplated the image. It was almost a poem. Her grandparents, her mother's parents, were buried in a garden-like cemetery under a maple tree, a flowerbed in front of their headstones. That was back east where they still did that kind of thing. When she visited there with her mother, Ella, Mom back then, her mother planted peonies there, squatting on her knees. A bird sang out, a blue bird. "Mating," her mother said. In a pond nearby two white swans glided together. When they'd passed the pond in the car her mother said, "They mate for life." And death, Beatriz thought, reminiscing now, and then it ends, finally and for good. She wished that you could open a grave like you could a book, wondered whether her parents would be buried or cremated.

When she returned to the bookstore to retrieve her flashlight and pad, Christina was gone. She locked up and followed the flashlight beam through the dark halls, out the back door and through the garden to the dark door of the buried library. The door was metal, flat gray, windowless; it had a metal handle, too, not a doorknob. There was a lock above the handle, but she had no key. That could end things. But she pushed down on the handle, and it moved. When she pushed the door with her shoulder, though stiff and resistant, the door creaked open. She peaked inside. Her flashlight went out. She stepped back outside.

When the flashlight wouldn't relight, she struck a match, raised the glass surrounding the lantern wick and lit the lantern. Light splayed faintly, almost uselessly, into the stacks. She reached back to hold the door ajar, to let in some air and light, but, as well, she feared it might slam behind her and trap her inside. She thought of turning back but felt something drawing her inside too. The air, which she expected to smell of rot and mold, was somehow verdant. Still, she stood at the entrance, her palm holding the door handle. She heard a voice. A woman's voice. It said, softly, You'll have to shut the door.

Her mind flashed. If she couldn't see who was speaking, then the voice might be in her head. Moreso, like in the movies, she was a young woman, alone, going into a dark basement with only a candle to investigate a noise. Time to back up and walk away. Or at least get up from her seat and walk out of the theater.

Had a few minutes passed? An hour?

Close the door, repeated the voice. It wasn't a whisper, but neither demanding nor threatening, neither was it *in* her head. It came from somewhere in the stacks. A woman's voice, almost a song. Beatriz raised her lantern, but its light failed to penetrate the catacomb.

If you don't come in and shut the door, all the stories here will disappear.

"And you?" said Beatriz.

And me. No light from your world can penetrate this one.

She felt both frightened and curious, like a foal standing in front of a corral gate accidently left ajar, trembling in front of an unknown world. She'd never had this feeling before.

She thought to test the door from outside, to see if it might lock behind her from within. Again, she stepped back.

If you step out now, said the voice, I will never again be here for you. But if you shut the door and put out your lantern, you'll prove your trust. You'll be safe and later can come and go as you please.

But what was such a promise worth? At her back, the night, before her, Darkness and a voice. Common sense told her to play it safe, to choose the night. But she suddenly saw her life up to that moment as a series of choices to back away. She would back away again, into what? She turned and shut the door. Extinguished the worthless lantern as the door latch clicked behind her. She faced the Darkness.

II

As when you awaken in a dark room, in time your eyes adjust and the things around you slowly become apparent. Objects arise like shadows. This is the time for ghosts. She remembered, in her cottage, sitting up in bed and seeing two cats playing on her clothes chest. She didn't own cats. She couldn't make out their colors or markings, the light was too gray, but a thin cat sat upon the chest and a fluffy one below. They batted at each other in that aggressive, playful way of cats. They made no sounds. She closed her eyes. Waited. Opened them. The cats were still there, completely real and totally unreal. She lay down and fell asleep. In the morning there were no cats.

For the next two nights she set her inner clock to awaken in the dark, and for the next two nights she saw the cats. Then, on the fourth night, they didn't appear. They never came again.

III

In the underground library, as if awakening in the dark, the stacks and nooks took form, but it was more than just her eyes adjusting to the dark, it was as if every stack, every book exclaimed its own transcendental light. In the aisle in front of her, a young woman stood. She had light auburn hair, pulled back, brown eyes, her cheeks were full, if though not round, they displayed an array of tiny scars, remnants of pocks, it seemed. She wore a narrow-waisted brown silk dress that fell from her waist to the floor, her shoulders exposed.

"Who are you?" said Beatriz.

"I am Mary Wollstonecraft Godwin . . . Shelley."

"Like the girl who wrote *Frankenstein*," Beatriz said.

The young woman didn't answer her but turned and walked into the illumined aisle of books.

Beatriz followed, then stopped. Every book on every shelf, whether wide or thin, had the same inscription on its spine. *John Keats*. Mary turned to her, but only part way, speaking over her right shoulder.

"Obviously, she said, "you start with Keats."

It wasn't obvious at all to Beatriz why she would start with Keats. Why not, if they were being obvious, as if there were anything obvious in this circumstance, why not Shelley? Or Mary Shelley? It seemed in every instant that the rules of common sense were falling away.

"Can I leave?" said Beatriz.

Mary turned to face her. "Of course you can leave."

"The door won't be locked?"

"The door was never locked."

"You'll be here?"

"That's a more difficult question to answer," Mary Shelley said. "I never really know where or when I'll be anywhere. Does anyone?"

"Can I bring others?" Beatriz said.

"I can almost assure you that if you bring others it will be very different. Everyone creates their own reality. This is yours."

"Mine alone."

"We are born alone. We live alone. We die alone. If we come back, we come back alone. We are all monsters," Mary Shelley said.

"Monsters," said Beatriz.

"It's frightening," Mary Shelley said.

Beatriz couldn't tell. She was too confused to be frightened. She gathered up her things. "I'll be back," she said.

When she opened the cellar door to the garden it was daylight, the garden in autumn bloom, the citrus trees, orange and grapefruit, lime and lemon, tangerine, yet hung with fat late fruit, artichokes sprouted from their bushes, red hibiscus flowers and purple bougainvillea blossomed in the slanting October morning light, fat-leafed giant elephant ears brushed against her waist as she walked. How long had she been below? Time had leapt, though she didn't recall falling asleep or waking up. The bookstore was open and empty but for Christina Acevedo, who sat working at her desk. She looked up from her laptop. Her fingernails were painted red. She wore red lipstick.

"Coming to work?" said Christina.

"I'm afraid I've been down below all night," Beatriz said.

"All night?"

"Since you left," said Beatriz. "Has anyone on the Board been down there?"

"It was dark. The flashlights didn't work," said Christina. She closed her laptop and her red nails glared atop the silver case.

"The lantern didn't work either," Beatriz said to her. "It lit, but the light didn't penetrate."

"All night?" said Christina.

"What did Lee see?"

"He didn't. He heard voices. That was enough for him."

"Men's?" said Beatriz. "Women's?"

"He didn't say. They were indiscernible," said Christina.

"So how did he know they were voices?"

"The imagination can be a terrible thing," said Christina Acevedo.

"You've been there," said Beatriz.

Christina took a deep breath, exhaled heavily. "Have a seat," she said. "Were you dreaming?"

"I didn't fall asleep or wakeup."

"Was it a vision or a waking dream?" said Christina. "'Do I wake or sleep?'

That's Keats."

Beatriz sat down on the folding chair. "You saw Keats?" she said.

"More like Lee," said Christina. "I just felt something. Nothing threatening or harmful. But I haven't gone back."

"You sent me," said Beatriz.

"Yes, I'm too old."

Beatriz moved to the edge of her seat. She pressed down on it with her palms. She was on another precipice. "I saw someone," she said.

"Down there?"

"In the stacks." She told Christina about the odd illumination, the young woman. "She said if I didn't shut the door and come in, I might never be able to come back."

"A woman," said Christina. "She spoke to you? How old?"

"Her name was Mary Wollstonecraft Godwin Shelley. She looked my age, I think."

"Her age when Shelley died."

"Why me?" said Beatriz.

"Your age? Who knows what you saw or what you thought you saw."

"And heard," Beatriz said.

"So you stayed. All night."

"When I went in it was evening, but when I came out it was daylight. Yet it felt like a short time."

"Did you see anyone else?" said Christina.

Beatriz merely shook her head, slightly, slowly. "No."

Christina stood and retrieved a bottle of pale liquid from the shelves behind her desk. It was stored behind her books. She opened a desk drawer and brought out two small tulip shaped glasses and filled the bottom of each. She handed one to Beatriz. "Sherry," she said.

"Isn't it morning?" Beatriz said.

"Time," said Christina. "Really? In other countries, less obsessed with drunkenness, people drink day and night. You need this." She raised her glass to Beatriz and sipped.

Beatriz sipped too. It was sweet up front but burned slightly going down. "You know something," she said to Christina, barely louder than a whisper.

"You should eat something," Christina said.

"I could leave for good, like Lee," Beatriz said.

Christina sipped again and stared deeply into Beatriz' eyes. "How could you?" she said.

That night she looked up Mary Shelley on the internet but was informed that information on Mary Shelley was "currently unavailable." To her memory, never before had that ever happened. As well, she hadn't read *Frankenstein*. She looked for it on several book websites, but even Amazon didn't have it. She did find one book by Mary Shelley, a novel entitled *The Last Man*, a lengthy book with cumbersome, challenging prose. She thought again of her encounter with the woman in the underground library. If a dream, even a waking dream, it seemed harmless enough, though the most benevolent dream could turn monstrous in an instant. "We are all monsters," the young woman had said. Monsters dreaming, monsters dreaming monstrous dreams? Was this woman a ghost? Yet she appeared so fully embodied. And if a dream, wakeful or not, would it repeat or progress? She could be dreaming the whole world around her right now and dreamlike, dream a lifetime that passes in a moment. And then death.

Beatriz is literate, but admittedly young and not well-read. Her parents were readers and writers, but it hadn't made them happy or content, and she, in turn, surrounded by their books and scribbled musings, some of them published, preferred the singular anti-intellectualism of video games: try to jump from this roof to the next, miss, fall down, even die, but then come back to try again, finish, get all the way to the grail, or the secret word that destroys the monster; that's as complex as she wanted it to get.

Later that afternoon, when she showed up for her peculiar job, she asked Christina if the store had a copy of *Frankenstein*, about the monster.

Christina offered a bemused smile. "Dr. Frankenstein is the creator, not the monster," she said.

"I might have seen the movie when I was little," Beatriz said.

"There's a lot of them. Maybe there's a copy of the novel in the cellar," said Christina.

"Why don't you go down?"

Christina finished her sherry. "As I said, too old." She pushed her thick, black hair behind her shoulders. "Listen, just forget it."

That's when Beatriz realized she couldn't forget it.

When she entered the basement library that day, the walls lit up in ambient sepia. Mary Shelley stepped out from behind the nearest stacks. She said, "Welcome back."

"Well at least this proves I didn't make it up," said Beatriz.

"It neither proves nor disproves," said Mary. "All realities are peculiar, don't you think? Yet ours have crossed."

"Are you a ghost?" said Beatriz.

"Are you a ghost?" said Mary Shelley.

Beatriz tried to recall what she knew, or what she thought she knew, about ghosts. Those cats playing in her bedroom. Once, some years ago, on a ski vacation with her family in Park City, Utah, her grandmother, her mother's mother, now dead, said a man appeared at the foot of her bed; he wore 19th century attire, a gray suit, a buttoned down vest and a wide tie. He smoked a cigarette. She watched. He silently smoked. Then frightened, she shut her eyes.

"Do you believe in ghosts?" Beatriz' father had asked her.

"No," she said. "What kind of world would have ghosts in it?"

Beatriz' father, Wil, surmised that she had awakened into half-consciousness, half awake and half dreaming.

"I was frightened, but he didn't hurt me," her grandmother said. But when it happened again the next night she wouldn't go back in the room. Beatriz' father and mother traded rooms with Grandma. No one saw the ghost again, though one day, returning from breakfast, they found the balcony door, which they thought they'd locked, cracked open. On the dining table, a local magazine lay open to a story about a miner with an old photo of a man dressed very much like Grandma's ghost. The story about him was vague and confusing but said the miner had been the owner of the land where the condo now stood. Mysteriously, he was swindled out of the land, then murdered.

"That's ghost stories for you," Ella said. "Are you afraid?" she asked her young daughter.

"I don't know," Beatriz answered.

"I am," her grandmother said.

Nonetheless, they moved to another apartment.

"I am a traveler," Mary Shelley said to Beatriz. "Until now, I've travelled through my life again and again. If I've ever haunted anyone, it's been myself."

"Now is two hundred years later," said Beatriz.

"I know nothing of what has happened since my death." She paused. "1854."

"And you don't know why."

"To guide you?" After some silence she said, "Why are you here?"

Beatriz wished she had a beer or a glass of wine. Something to buoy her. "I'm supposed to make a record of what's in the basement."

"I mean really, the bigger picture."

"To live my life, I suppose."

"Burden enough," said Mary Shelley. "Follow me." She turned to the Keats stacks. There it was, floor to ceiling, volumes of John Keats on both sides, an alleyway, an allegory, never ending.

"This is all John Keats?" Beatriz asked.

"More Keats than ever there was."

"Why Keats?"

"Because we start with Keats."

"Not before?"

"Do you mean Coleridge or Wordsworth? Or my father, Godwin, or Mary Wollstonecraft?"

Beatriz didn't know. They were mere names to her. She didn't know their lives or work. "Kubla Kahn?" she said.

"Through caverns measureless to man," said Mary Shelley. "If you don't die young, you die drunken, drugged and old." She turned to Beatriz. "If you want truth and beauty, follow me. If you want knowledge, go back to school."

"That's why me," said Beatriz.

"That's why we start here." Mary turned again and spread her arms.

IV

A light fell down at the end of the aisle, ephemeral, not like real light, laying down like the white wing of a bird, a swan; she felt a warm, summer wind; for a moment thought she heard birdsong, for a moment felt like a fledgling beneath her mother's soft, feathered breast. She turned around to look for Mary, but Mary was gone.

She turned again. A man appeared before her, not ten feet away. He sat at a small writing desk, gently bathed in the soft light. Feathered pen in hand, he raised his head. His eyes were dark, his hair dark too, long enough to touch his neck, wavy, neither straight nor curly, his face white and poignant with a distinctive, strong, bluntly pointed nose. "Come closer," he said. "My outer vision is not so good, though already I can see deep inside you."

"Inside me," said Beatriz, in barely a whisper.

"Beauty finds its way," the young man said. He stood. He wasn't tall, shorter than her.

"Are you John Keats?" Beatriz said. "A ghost from the past?"

"Are you a ghost from the future?" he said. He stepped toward her; his palms upturned. "Life is but a day," he said softly. "A fragile dewdrop on its perilous way." He offered her a slight smile. "I can see you now. You have blue eyes."

"Like Fanny," she said. She didn't even know why she said it. She didn't know who Fanny could be. As if somehow someone else was speaking inside her.

"Regrettably," he said, "we go to heaven alone. We come back from heaven alone."

They were no longer in the basement library, but on a trail on the side of a mountain. A breeze chilled her, though now she wore a wool hat and coat, thick, laced boots. The boulders and cliffs around them were black. Tall, bright brown fir trees swayed, oddly the same color as the diffuse library light.

"Larches," said Keats. "We'll need to move more quickly if we want to find an inn by sunset."

He walked forward. She followed.

"Listen," he said. Small birds flapped and twittered amidst the trees, then the whirling and gush of a brook. "I will show you a torrent of flowers and stars, a sky melting into roses. And you, my Fanny Braun."

"These cliffs," said Beatriz.

"The castles of Titans to fend the battling Gods."

"I'm not Fanny," she said.

"Yet here you are. The inn is just over the hill."

In front of a thatched cottage stood a little donkey; on his back pots and pans clattered when he shook. Inside, people, mostly men, chattered in a language she couldn't understand.

"Gaelic," said Keats.

"Ireland?"

"Scotland."

They ate oat cakes and hard-boiled eggs, ale, some whisky and water from metal cups. The lighting was candlelight. She knew they were somewhere else now, somewhen else.

"You've been here before," she said to him.

Keats sipped from his cup. The innkeeper threw a log on the fireplace fire. "I search for old companions. I feel somehow, I might meet them again."

"But you never do?"

He coughed, then wheezed. "It's a foolish choice to come back from the dead, because you return to life, then you must, as well, return to death, but the same life, and the same death."

"But the library," said Beatriz.

"Yes, something is different this time, the library . . . and you. Are you Fanny?"

"I am not Fanny."

"How do you know? What if I say that I am not John Keats? What would that change?"

There was one small straw mattress in an upstairs room. They slept on it together, clothes on. Once, during the night, he laid his arm over her back, coughed, awoke, and turned away, their backs touching. They had an egg in the morning with tea, though she would have preferred coffee. She told him that. "This is England, Scotland," he said. "You have a peculiar accent."

She said, "America."

"Where they kill the native Indians."

She grimaced. But she wondered that he wasn't more curious. He seemed driven by other things.

"I am," he said, as if he could read her thoughts. "I see deeper. I look for the deeper. Maybe you have come, this time, to help me find it."

"Or for me to find it," she said. Again, she felt as if she were speaking from someone else. Were they both ghosts?

Then they headed out again toward where he said there were ruins of an old monastery. She followed his footsteps through a living forest verdant with the rustling of birds and branches, a forest that she felt increasingly inseparable from her senses, here, alive amidst all life. It then appeared almost out of nowhere, a kind of low-slung castle, crumbling, around a crumbling steeple, its archways covered in moss and vines.

"Come," said Keats, and he led her through the ruined abbey, through winding passageways, aisles, and galleries, cloisters, pillars, shattered encasements where hung the remnants of ancient window frames, arched doorways, and the sad, faded, partial effigies of martyred saints.

"This is a poem," he said. "They didn't know they were building and living in the space between eternity and nothing. When I write, I start with the nothing and let eternity emerge."

"How old?" said Beatriz.

"I imagine it was destroyed and pilfered when Henry VIII left the Roman Church." He brought out a flask and offered her a drink. She took it. It tasted a bit like the liquor that Christina gave her. When she handed it back to him, he toasted her and drank.

"When is it now?" she asked. "Not 2025."

"1818?" he said.

"We traveled in time?"

"You can't travel in time," Keats said to her. "We travel inside what we are, what we were. No more."

"Mary Shelley said that, too."

"Mary Shelley?"

"In the library."

"Maybe it's a place of exception. A nexus of exception. In time, which is everywhere always."

Now she heard a kind of humming, rhythmic, dirge-like. The walls breathed. A figure emerged from behind the debris that was once a marble altar. A woman in a brown robe and veil. Then another followed her, hands folded. Beatriz had no name for their clothes, long robes that stretched to the floor, white collars, rosaries wrapped around their waists. Did they walk or float? Now more followed. They turned and together faced the visitors.

"Do you see them?" said Beatriz.

"Only through *your* eyes," said Keats. He began to perspire.

Though they appeared to sing, no sound came from their mouths, yet the ancient walls vibrated with a melodic, song-like buzz.

"I can't hear them," said Beatriz.

"It would be Latin," he said. "But ghosts can't speak. So, you see, I'm not a ghost."

"Nor I," said Beatriz. "Then what's singing?"

"Ambience," said Keats.

She took a step toward the ghostly chorus.

"They don't see you!" he said.

The floating figures spread out their arms. On their backs, brown, feathered wings formed as the group began to blend into one another until slowly they became a solitary winged being that continued to shrink until only one small creature hung in front of Beatriz and Keats, a light brown bird with a short, orange beak. It began to sing, a short, pretty wurp, followed by a chirp, then a call, then a chatter, a pause, and it began again.

"You said ghosts didn't speak," she said.

"He isn't speaking but singing. He's singing to you, Fanny, Beatriz. I see now why we came here, to hear this nightingale sing to you in this eternal twilight."

"Eternal," said Beatriz.

He put a finger on her lips. "Not sounds at all, but musical thoughts, the feel of nothing, pushing back."

When they re-entered the forest, the day had grown late and dark; she felt the limbs of the trees reach upward to the overcast sky reaching down, she didn't just see them, she felt them.

"It's going to rain," he said, and led her to a clearing where stood a small, wooden shack, straw spread across the floor. He made a bed of it and bid her lie down next to him. And thoughtlessly, she did. He stretched out next to her and gently placed his hand on hers. Not knowing where she was or when she was, she heard the rain patter on the roof and partly dreamed she was in heaven.

"No," he said, "rather awake forever in a sweet unrest."

They awakened at dawn to a canopy of birdsong; in the open air she felt what she saw and touched what she heard; her body filled with bliss.

"The birds," she said to Keats.

"Each of them filled with heaven," he said.

"You?"

"William Blake. He said it better."

"'Tyger Tyger'," Beatriz said.

"You know more than you profess," said Keats.

"Grade school," she said.

"Watch," he said. He put out his hand and a sparrow alighted on his forefinger.

"You've done that before," she said.

"But not with you. Take her," he said to Beatriz, and placed the little bird on her cupped hands. "I am that bird," he said to her.

Embarrassed, she thought to divert him. "In two hundred years sparrows will be extinct in England," she said.

"But that isn't now," replied Keats. "This bird is alive now."

Truly, his poetry could not be diverted.

They walked and walked on narrow roads and narrower paths, a cascade of trees around them like a breathing tunnel. She could no longer tell one day from another, nor how many nights. He took her hand. And Beatriz sang:

And when you ran to me
Your cheeks flushed with the night
We walked in frosted fields
Of juniper and lamplight
I held your hand

"Is that your song?" he said.

"No. You made me think of it. I don't sing often, with anyone or to anyone."

"Juniper and lamplight. Thank you, Fanny."

"Beatriz."

"When I made this trek before, I did it with a friend, but I didn't make it to the Loch of Inverness. I fell ill and caught a boat home. But this time, with you, I dream I'll make it."

They came to a river and began following it through the black Scottish cliffs.

"This is the Inverness River," said Keats. "You have changed my destiny." His brow perspired. He suppressed a cough. "I'm emptying my heart now, so you and angels may enter."

She didn't know if she'd ever been in love, ever fallen in love. She thought not. Was she falling now, two hundred years ago, with this black eyed deep hearted poet?

"Beyond love," he said, again answering her thoughts.

"The song," she said, "is from my parents' time. You were a Romantic."

"I yet am."

"When they were young there was a war."

"There are always wars. Some are wrong. Some are necessary."

"I've read a little about you. You backed Napoleon."

"We are against hereditary rule, royalty, kings. At least he wasn't a king."

"My parents marched, sang songs, were vegetarians. My father refused conscription. They sided with the Blacks, the American Indians. They despised authority, corporations, industrial pollution."

"I imagine they failed," Keats said.

"I suppose. I suppose they did." Odd, that she thought of them now, how they'd lived for causes. How that waned. How ideals waned. The world waned.

The river started to push harder now, smashing black against the rocks; it bashed out the smells of the forest, the pines and the leaves, different from the power of the ocean, more swift and univocal, threatening, active, erasing contemplation.

"We'll get by these rapids and find a quiet, soft spot under a tree," he said. "We should make the loch tomorrow."

They found that tree, a big beech, and softened a spot beneath it with wild grass. Now the river murmured, soothing and reassuring. He still had brandy and they sipped it; they faced each other, legs crossed, touching knee to knee.

"You brought biscuits," he said.

She retrieved two from her pack and gave him one.

"You read about me," he said. "Where?"

"It was an encyclopedia, not a book, but on a screen, an electronic screen."

"Electricity," he said. "We know it's coming. Did you read any poems?"

She let her hair down. She figured that in this time and place mature women didn't do that in public, but it felt good on her neck and ears. A release. She shook her hair. He smiled.

"I couldn't understand them." She paused. "The bird in the convent. A nightingale?"

"Yes," he said. "You've seen the title. Now read the poem."

"And 'Grecian Urn', 'Beauty is truth, truth beauty, that's all you need to know'."

He laughed, delighted, and it delighted her. "If you go back to it," he said, "read it backwards. You are beauty and truth. That's why you're here." He ran his right hand through her hair and touched her cheek. Above them, in the tree, birds flapped, settling into the dusk. They listened. Then he said, "That odd state of soul in which the void becomes eloquent."

"Are you writing poems now?" said Beatriz?

"In any moment."

"In the library?"

"Yes. Always writing. Always chasing the world away."

"Could I see it?

"No. No one will ever see it."

"Written on water," she whispered.

"You've read more than you admit," he said.

He reached for his pack and lay back on it. She did the same, lying next to him. The wind in the leaves. The water rushing behind.

He spoke softly to the air:

When I have fears that I may cease to be

Before my pen has gleaned my teeming brain,

Before high-piled books, in charactery,

Hold like rich garners the full ripen'd grain;

When I behold upon the night's starr'd face,

Huge cloudy symbols of a high romance,

And think that I may never live to trace

Their shadows with the magic hand of chance;

And when I feel, fair creature of an hour

That I never live to look upon thee more,

Never have relish in the faery power

Of unreflecting love;—then on the shore

Of the wide world I stand alone, and think

That love and fame to nothingness do sink.

The air around them quieted. They touched hands. "You just made love to me," she said

He said, "Yes."

In the morning they followed the river again. It began to spread out wider and shallower, until it opened to a vast, gray lake. As they walked to a black sand beach, a cold wind swept over them. It didn't take long for a bank of low, purple clouds to form to the north and more morbidly over the water. Beneath it Beatriz spotted a black speck gliding. "Look," she said. "Fish don't float."

"Something else," said Keats.

"Something else? What could it be?"

"A boat?"

The object moved resolutely before the storm. She couldn't discern a sail. Beatriz said, "Should we turn back?"

"I think we're safer right here," he said. "Facing it. Are you frightened?"

She said nothing but moved closer to him. The waves picked up as the wind howled. He put his arms around her. The object disappeared beneath the waves.

"There," he said. "There. The storm will pass over us. They always do."

She shivered. She tried to put this together. How was she here? What could come next? What would be left for them when the storm passed, for her, in the wilderness of Scotland with a dying young poet, two hundred years ago.

They braced against the first cold sheets of rain. Something roared, but it didn't come from the sky. The loch stirred and bubbled before them. The head of something emerged, large gray eyes, a skull flat and black. Then, simultaneously, a body rose up upon a pair of huge fins. The head danced atop a long neck. It let out both a roar and scream as it opened its maw, lined with a jaw of jagged pointed teeth like knives. She clutched Keats closer as the animal thrust itself toward them. It screamed again. The lake and sky crashed.

"Empty your heart," Keats said to her.

And then they disappeared inside the blackness.

V

She stood in front of Christina.

"You were down below for quite a while," Christina said.

"A while?"

"All afternoon."

"I've been gone for weeks," said Beatriz.

"Weeks," said Christina.

Beatriz said, "I was with Keats."

"Keats." Christina got up and walked in front of her desk. She took both of Beatriz' hands.

"In Scotland."

Christina looked deeply into her eyes. "Have you been there before?"

"No," said Beatriz.

"You took a plane?"

"It was 1818."

"Maybe sherry's not the drink for you," Christina said.

"We drank ale, and brandy."

"You and Keats." Christina retrieved her cell phone from her purse. She called up her calendar and showed it to Beatriz. "Do you see the date? October 11. That's today. The day you came to work. Today." Once again, she held Beatriz hands. "You dreamed," she said.

"I didn't dream. We hiked." She squeezed Christina's hands. "You know something," she said to her.

Christina shook her head.

She didn't tell Christina about the monster. She drove home. From outside, she watched her mother and father, under candlelight, touching hands, sipping wine. She thought of the untold caverns and tunnels of their lives. Now she had some of her own, wondered if each life was torn by freedom and spirit, passion, and conviction. Had they ever shared a day or a month walking and talking with Camus or Proust? What did it mean to open a book? Should she go back?

Neither Mary Shelley nor Keats had opened a book for her. She thought of her circle of friends who had now fallen away, most drastically when she quit high school, though they had fallen away from each other as well, fallen into college or marriage or jobs; some had moved to other countries, maybe that's what she was doing now, falling into another country, or if they'd fallen into cyber-worlds, into screens, what was more real? Though she didn't want to fall into that labyrinth of chasing the really real, if it had not now already found her; what had Keats said as they entered the monster's maw? Empty your heart. She looked to the window again. Only her father, Wil, sat there now, his face complicated by candlelight. Her mother now stood beside her. She held two glasses of wine and offered one to Beatriz, who took it.

"What's wrong?" her mother said.

Her mother, Ella, was yet beautiful. Her hair, gray-blonde, fell to her shoulders, her eyes, unlike Beatriz', were green, her skin sallow, she wore a gray shirt-dress that fell to her knees over black tights.

"I don't know anything about you," Beatriz said.

"What is there ever to know?" Ella said, "stories, gossip, lies."

"Is that why you quit teaching?"

"You're like your father," said Ella, "you cut right to the quick. There were a hundred reasons. Overdetermined. Do you know that term?"

"Not really."

"Freud."

"A sexist," said Beatriz.

"So you throw out everything?"

"And Dad?"

"A very underappreciated intellect and writer," said her mother.

They both looked to the window where Beatriz' father sat, alone. Faintly, you could hear a piano. Bill Evans. Beatriz didn't listen to jazz, nor pop or hip-hop.

"How's work?" her mother asked.

"They discovered a basement library behind the main building. I'm to catalogue its contents."

"Are they paying you?"

Beatriz didn't respond. Her parents had told her she could do what she wanted with her life and they would try to support her. They probably didn't suspect that she would do nothing. But time flew. The pandemic had closed a lot of doors.

"It's oddly fulfilling," she said to her mother.

"More than selling coffee and donuts."

"Yes," Beatriz said. She couldn't really say much more. What could she say? "Do you know Mary Shelley?"

"She wrote *Frankenstein* when she was only nineteen. Have you read it?"

"I should," said Beatriz.

"Is it in your library?" Ella said.

Beatriz said, "That's hard to say. I haven't found it."

"I'll get you a copy," said her mother. "Another, *The Last Man*, is about the final survivor of a pandemic."

"Kind of prescient," Beatriz said.

"She was, in so many ways," said her mother. She finished her wine, as did Beatriz. "I just wanted to make sure you were okay."

"That's hard to say, too," said Beatriz. "That library. Maybe I'm finding myself there."

VI

Mary Shelley stood in front of her at the mouth of an aisle of shelves filled with Percy Bysshe Shelley's books. She held a package. It was in brown paper, wrapped and folded. Her face was calm, her eyes shining, penetrating. Slowly, she began to unfold the paper, meticulously shaping it into a bowl. "Percy Shelley's heart," she said. "He died in a shipwreck. Edward Trelawny, Leigh Hunt, and Byron found his remains on shore and cremated him. But his heart didn't burn. Hunt took his ashes to Rome to be buried next to Keats, but he kept Percy's heart. I begged him for it for ten years until he finally relented and gave it to me."

"You weren't there?"

"I was home, with Jane, the wife of Williams, the other man who drowned. There was a cabin boy too, never found. Jane Williams loved Percy. We all did. You had to."

She slowly opened the package that she held and a cloud of heart ash floated between them.

VII

Yet the ashes didn't fall at their feet but danced in the air, and lifted by an inexplicable breeze, spread in size and floated down the Shelley aisle to the bottom of a wooden ladder. The library light dimmed. The floor rolled back and forth. Mary climbed the ladder and Beatriz followed her to the deck of a ship.

It's a gentle day with the same gentle breeze filling the ship's sails, pushing the boat on a mild sea. The wind pushes Beatriz' ankle-length skirt against her legs. They are approaching land.

"Calais," says Mary. "Percy will meet us. With Claire."

"Claire?" says Beatriz.

"Clairton. Is my stepsister. We're going to Italy with Shelley."

"Shelley isn't dead?" Beatriz said.

"Not now," said Mary. "Not here. Here he will sail. He will write great poems in this paradise and we will copy them down."

Mary looked even younger now. Her eyes and skin as clear as a child's.

"What about his cremation?"

"I'm afraid I don't know what you're talking about," Mary said. "I'm so excited."

Beyond confusion, Beatriz watched as the ship made harbor. A young man and a much younger girl waved to them. There was shouting on the boat as sailors dropped sail and caught ropes thrown from the pier. Mary went below and returned once, then twice, toting large sacks with canvas handles. She gave one to Beatriz. "Our things," Mary said.

"Where did we meet?" said Beatriz.

"In a library?" said Mary Shelley. "At the end of time?"

"Can I go back?"

"Who's to know," Mary said. "To where? Things tend to move forward, don't they? Here we are, in France, with the greatest poet alive!"

"Not Keats?" said Beatriz

Mary hugged her and laughed. "Oh, maybe Keats. Not Byron! What does it matter?"

Yet it all mattered very much to Beatriz. The air swirled around her. A sailor took her arm and led her to the gang plank, following Mary. Percy leapt to Mary and the two of them kissed and hugged, then Percy stepped back and held Mary at arm's length. He sighed so deeply that it felt, everywhere, as if the world had escaped from his chest. "Sheer joy," he said softly, "we are here together, the children of love." His eyes shone a brilliant silver-blue and his hair fell in waves to his neck. He glanced toward Beatriz, then looked back at Claire, then looked at Beatriz again, his brow framing a question.

"My cosmic friend, Beatriz," Mary said to him.

"Like Dante?" he said.

"If you must," said Mary.

Percy reached for Claire and in a simple gesture embraced the three young women. Impossibly, Beatriz felt a warm shiver run through her body, settling in her heart. In some eternal moment, Beatriz fell in love with him, with all of them; the beat of her heart was the heartbeat of the world. She would feel that, she knew, whenever he touched her. And then, as immediately, she felt the world around them full of terror and death, and Shelley, whispering in her ear, "That's why we must never look away from each other; we live, now, on the divide between infinite love and eternal moments of horror."

He led them to a carriage pulled by two bays. Mary and Beatriz took the seats inside, Shelley sat in the driver's seat with Claire and let her take the reins.

"She's the daughter of my father's second wife," Mary said to Beatriz.

"You're not jealous?" asked Beatriz.

"She's quite good with horses," said Mary.

Out the window Beatriz watched as they swept past a lighthouse, then moved through the streets of the old city of Calais, leaving the sea smell of fish markets for the clatter of commerce and brick buildings, then through the city gates into the countryside.

"How old are you?" she asked Mary.

"Sixteen," she said. "Like you."

"Like me?" said Beatriz. "I'm afraid I'm nineteen."

"Claire just turned sixteen."

"Didn't Percy die in a shipwreck?"

"You're quite the dreamer," said Mary. "Percy is divorcing his wife who lives in London. He will marry me. And we will begin our own dream life in Italy."

Claire guided the carriage into the stable yard where she and Percy dismounted and he helped Mary, then Beatriz, step down from the carriage. Percy hugged Mary passionately. "I suppose you're coming along," he eventually said to Beatriz. "Gather your things. We can't afford to live like tourists. Cologne is just down the road. We can bed there and then be off."

They gathered their things. Beatriz had a bag of her own. Percy gave each girl a small jug of water and a boiled egg, then they headed down the road, single file, Percy, Mary, Claire, then Beatriz. They walked between fields of purple heather, golden-brown barley, and wheat. It was a pretty day, the sun gentle overhead. There were occasional streams, spanned by wooden bridges, ponds frequented by ducks and long-necked white birds, egrets, and swans. Farmers drove wagons pulled by horses, but no machines. Beatriz didn't want to play the fool, even to herself. She guessed she was in someone else's dream, maybe Mary's, and as with Keats, the early 19th century. From something inside herself, here, in this now, she felt sixteen. Up ahead, Shelley began to hum some kind of folk song; it sounded like something a rock band, The Lumineers? might sing, but when was that? She was a child and barely listened even then. Mary joined in, harmonizing, Claire did not. She walked solemnly, preoccupied. After a while they rested under a birch, near a pond. They ate their eggs. Percy broke bread. They passed the loaf around. Shelley removed his boots and socks and stood in the shallow water. He spread his arms and yelled, "I love the water, but I can't swim!"

When he turned to the girls, Beatriz said, "Why don't you learn?"

Everyone laughed.

Percy said, "I don't want to do everything Byron does! I don't want to do *anything* Byron does!"

But Mary whispered to her, "They both love to sail," and giggled.

She didn't know that he would die on the water in a storm? That Byron would help bury him? Who was this young Mary? Was she not the woman in the basement library? How many times could life fold back upon itself, in living, in dreaming, in memory, in lives forgiven and forgotten?

Could it be that she was sixteen? Could you feel the difference between being sixteen and nineteen? Only if you were once nineteen first. Later, when they had paused in the dusk and found shelter in a barn attached to an inn, a woman, the wife of the innkeeper, brought them a cauldron of bean soup, bowls and spoons, metal mugs filled with hard cider. She spoke to Shelley in French, sometimes English. She refused his offer to pay.

"I know who you are," she said. She turned her head, taking in the three girls who sat around him. She turned to Shelley again. "You are a river of legend, without destination or source."

"The river of time," said Percy.

"Rolls not forward but back and forth."

"How can she know him?" Beatriz whispered to Mary.

"He's been here before," Mary said to her, exploding, in a moment, what in another moment, appeared quite miraculous.

The woman gathered up the cups and bowls. When she came to Beatriz, who held her cup close to her chest for a last sip; their fingers touched; their eyes held each other's eyes.

"Tu es nouveau," said the woman, Beatriz not realizing that she'd used the intimate, not the formal form of address. "Not new this time, but completely new."

That night Shelley came to each of them separately, beginning with Mary and ending with Beatriz. He lay down beside her, facing her.

"I can't explain why I'm here," she said to him.

"Because you've met Keats."

"Did I?"

"I feel him in you," Percy said, "or around you. Did you make love to him?"

Beatriz propped her head on her hand. "That's difficult to say."

Shelley laughed. "That's Keats all right. Well," he said, "it's already remembered in eternity. But because we're always there, it's easy to forget. Are you coming with us to Italy?"

For a moment, now she remembers, or conjures, that she read this in a book, at the end of a long row of books, on a page, there, in the library's sepia light, she lies with Shelley.

"Do you love Mary?" she asks him.

"Mary is my true love. I met her over her mother's grave."

"Mary Wollstonecraft."

"Why yes. Fated to meet, and begin there, with death. Her mother, the wife of Mary's father, though neither believed in marriage. She died in giving birth to Mary."

"You're married," said Beatriz.

"And I don't believe in marriage either. But a woman alone in this world, legally alone, is the earth without sky."

"Yet you sleep with Claire."

"You're precocious," Shelley said. "Claire needs me. Anyone can make love to anyone. Where is marriage in these woods? What is love but the only thing.

The rest is fear, hope, waste, death." He touched her cheek. "I'm going back to Mary now."

She slept through the night, dreaming she was dreamless.

In the morning Shelley sprained his ankle on a tree root. Outside Reims he rented a donkey and a cart, after a day of drinking champagne. In this way, one of the girls at the reins with Shelley at her side, the other two walking on either side of the donkey, they pressed on toward Switzerland.

Beatriz learned to turn and guide the donkey—they named him Oro—with the reins and to move him forward from behind with the whip when he stopped and honked in his ugly donkey bray; she tapped the animal's hind end and cooed to him. Then he slowly moved forward, and Shelley laughed and cheered.

She knew, in the night, that he made love to Mary, and sometimes Claire, though he always awoke with Mary, and often he lay next to Beatriz, whispering, brimming with his ideals: a world without the petty and mean regress of religion and churches, the potential gentleness and generosity, the kindness and love of liberated men.

"And women," she said to him.

"Of course, my love," he answered.

But all was not ecstasy for Percy Bysshe Shelley. Physically frail, he often grew pale and coughed. His moods could shift wildly to uncontrolled sadness and grim, immobilizing depression. Whatever his passion for Mary Godwin, and Claire Clairton, he worried openly about his wife, Harriet, in London with their daughter and sickly son, claiming that it was her decision to leave him, over an infatuation with Byron. He was, in any moment, as likely to weep as laugh. He seemed to never have money, but somehow always had enough.

They made their way slowly through France, sleeping in barns or camping. They celebrated crossing to Switzerland, but found the Swiss response to their unusual travelling party tepid and stiff. But eventually they arrived in Neufchatel, that Shelley mistakenly thought was Italy. Nearby, in Brunnen, where the citizens spoke German, French, and Swiss, Shelley led them south to a body of water that he took to be Lake Lucerne.

"I think we're yet in Switzerland," Mary finally said to him.

"We have a big lake, mountains, I can write here," Shelley said.

Mary found a cottage on the water, and they moved in.

Shelley settled right in at a desk near a second-floor window with a view of the lake and the mountains beyond. Mary could sleep with him there, though sometimes, when Claire came to him, she shared a bed with Beatriz. There was a kitchen downstairs with a table, where they ate and Mary and Claire transcribed his morning output in the afternoons. Claire didn't cook and Beatriz didn't mind sharing that with Mary. Shelley rented a small sailboat with a single mast and indulged his passion for sailing. Mary found a telegraph office in a nearby village. Though he ate eggs and cheese, Shelley was a vegetarian and it was easy to find vegetables, rice, pasta, beer, and wine.

Beatriz couldn't read Shelley's handwriting, nor quite understand it when she could.

"Why not come sailing with me then?" said Percy.

"You should learn to swim," said Beatriz.

"I don't want to swim," he said. "I want to sail. For me, sky and wind!"

Beatriz was hesitant in a hundred ways, but within that lay only a few choices. Who was she now? And when? Was she truly new? Would she find herself as an unknown participant in someone's biography? If she went with him, could she die on some unknown Alpine lake? She was a good swimmer. Would that matter? This Mary. Yet Godwin now. Regardless, there was only the now, which in any time, in any reality, made no sense.

"I'm afraid for you," she said to him.

He gazed at her, his eyelids lowered, and briefly, he wept. "I'm touched," he whispered. "Come with me. Protect me."

She consulted Mary and Claire. Neither were interested in sailing in Percy's dinghy.

"Go with him," said Mary. "We'll be fine."

"There are fast storms on these lakes. Squalls," Claire said. "It's a small boat."

"He should learn to swim," Beatriz said.

The next day was glorious. The sun poured light on the lake that stretched to the horizon, as blue as the sky. Shelley took her hand as they walked the short green hill down to the dock, where the little skiff sat like a painting on the rippling lake.

"Did you write this morning?" Beatriz asked him.

"Of course. Do you know who Prometheus is?"

"He stole fire from the gods, to give to humanity."

"That's me," he said.

"A gift," she said. "For whom?"

"Now I'm just letting my soul out. But I must write to Harriet. Maybe Godwin. And Leigh Hunt."

She knew those names vaguely. He helped her on to the boat and seated her on a short bench, her back to the mast. He pushed off and quickly raised the sail, letting the breeze fill it and push them out.

"Gorgeous," he said. "Perfect. Wind at our backs, for now."

He worked behind her with the mast and tiller, guiding them into the lake, the water gushing against the prow. He reached for her and brought her back to him, showing her how moving the tiller in coordination with the sail guided the direction of the boat. Then he held her forearms and together they moved the boat from left to right and back again.

"All right now," he said, "a big turn," and they pushed the tiller and ducked under the swinging boom, he holding her arms again as she sailed them forty-five degrees to the right. They both laughed, the wind and water pushing at their faces. It was thrilling for her in every way, as their bodies pushed against each other, as in a dance.

"Fun?" he said.

"Yes," she said. "Yes!" She felt him securely around her, but neither affectionate nor threatening.

Percy held the tiller steady and let the wind pull them forward.

In the calm, she collected herself. "Did you love your wife?" Beatriz asked him.

"Still do," he said softly, as if his mind and heart were transported to another time and place. "She stopped loving me. We were both very young. She thought I would be more famous, and rich."

"You love Mary."

"More than anything. Sun and stars. Moonlight infinite."

"Enough to divorce and marry."

Shelley breathed heavily. "You're precocious and straightforward. I'm curious. Your accent."

"I'm from America," she said. "I'm nineteen."

"Keats has a brother there. Sometimes we dream of going. Starting a new world."

Shelley pointed to a dark bank of clouds on the forward horizon. "Something's coming," he said. "We best turn back."

He helped her turn the skiff around, but then took over. "We'll have to do some tacking," he said.

She returned to her seat at the base of the mast yet watched him over her shoulder as he moved the tiller and sailed back and forth, zig-zagging into the wind. Shelley labored a little but spoke between breaths as he ducked beneath the swiveling boom. "Society is ruled by greed, power, and men. Women are helpless because they have no money or power. Like Godwin, Mary's father, I don't believe in marriage, but if you love a woman, it's the only way to protect her."

Suddenly the wind dropped, and the air went completely still. The boat bobbed. Shelley looked about. The dark cloud bank loomed closer. When the breeze picked up again the wind shifted and came at their backs. Percy redirected the sail, but it became clear that they wouldn't outrun the approaching storm. He dropped the sail and wrapped it tightly around the mast. "We're going to have to ride it out," he said, just as the first cloud burst opened above them, releasing a heavy sheet of rain. Waves now rocked the boat. The sky became purple-black.

Shelley dove past Beatriz and flipping onto his back threw his hands and arms at the rails on the prow, as if he were crucified.

"Come here!" he yelled to Beatriz. "Lie back, between my legs."

Her head on his stomach, she reached for the boat rails, but she wasn't big enough, so placed her arms around each of his thighs. The boat rocked wildly. The rain slammed down like a wall as the waves bashed against them and on them.

"Will it fill?" Beatriz screamed.

"If it does, we're dead," he yelled back. "Or we could capsize, but that would kill us too."

"Bail?" she said.

"That might tip us. Just be still."

The rain poured down like bricks. The wind howled and the sky thundered and flashed. She began to cry, deep in her chest. A death wail. But how could they die? That she'd been alive *after* this meant nothing. The present reality was more real. Now Shelley screamed too. They were a chorus of fear and little else.

She wished she knew how to pray. She thought of her parents, two hundred years and thousands of miles away. Then came a flash of lightning, though this time the thunder followed more distantly. She turned to Shelley, who now stared almost blissfully at the sky. "Don't be afraid," he said. "The gods have died a million times."

"The gods!" she bleated.

"Changed nothing," he said.

Yet just as suddenly as the squall had stormed upon them, the rain let up, the wind died down, the waves sank. The sky opened.

They lay for a moment, then she turned and helped Percy to his knees. He stood unsteadily, then waded to a cabinet at the boat's stern and extracted two pails. "Now we bail," he said.

Without speaking, they dumped the water from the deck back into the lake. When it was down to a few inches, Shelley unleashed the sail as the sky rolled away from them. When they reached the dock, shivering and soaked, Mary was waiting there with woolen blankets. She wrapped each of her sojourners in one.

"I was very worried," she said.

"I was too," said Percy. "I thought only of you."

Mary retrieved a telegram from her bodice and gave it to Percy. He opened it. Looked up. "Harriet is dead," he said. "She drowned herself in the Serpentine."

That was the end of Italy. They packed up. Shelley found a boat and they set sail by river routes for the Channel. Beatriz remembers her fear of getting back on a boat. She remembers the mist and drizzle of the green Rhine. She gazes into the fog, but now it's the fog of Venice Beach. She stands outside the library, not ready to return. It's not late, but dusk. October dusk.

Inside the main building, Christina Acevedo greets her in the foyer. "You're all wet," she says. "You've been standing in the rain?"

"Over and over," Beatriz says. She's back in her 21st century shirt and jeans, yet she's all wet. She says, "Do you know who Claire Clairton is?"

"Was," says Christina. "Godwin's next daughter after Mary, after Wollstonecraft died."

"She walked across Europe with Percy and Mary," Beatriz says.

"You've been reading?" Christina asks.

Beatriz says: "Was it a vision, or a waking dream? Fled is that music.—Do I wake or sleep?"

"That's not Shelley," says Christina. "Did you read that?

"No," says Beatriz.

"It's 'Ode to a Nightingale.'"

"Keats recited it to me. It *was* a vision." She hesitates. Was she opening the doors to her madness? Yet she felt enlightened, clear, not mad, unless that was the feeling of madness. "Harriet Shelley drowned herself and her fetus in the Serpentine."

"Do you know what that is?"

"Shelley explained it."

Christina spoke very softly. "That happened a long time ago."

"That depends who you are and when you are," Beatriz said. "How long have I been gone?"

"A few days, at least."

"Over a month. I crossed France and Switzerland with the three of them."

Christina turned from her and walked toward the bookstore, stopping at the entrance. Then turned back toward her again. "You talk to them. Do you touch?"

"It's not a dream," said Beatriz. "It's not like a dream. Something is happening."

"To you," said Christina.

"Okay, yes, to me."

"If I go with you it won't happen."

"Are you asking me?" said Beatriz.

"I'm telling you," Christina said.

"So you know something."

"I know you could lose this job." Christina came to Beatriz again. "You don't have to go anymore."

"Someone else will go?"

"We'll work something out."

Would she sell tickets to readings? Organize the bookshelves by genre? She touched Christina's hand. It was time for a walk in the rain.

She left through the front doors and headed down Venice Blvd. The rain was more like a fine mist, a Los Angeles rain, merging the air and the sky, the air disappearing and the watery sky everywhere; it doesn't happen to you, you become it, a ghost in ghost air, what she first felt in the library, like a ghost, as Keats implied, that it was impossible to tell who the ghost was; to himself, he was who he was, when he was; she was his apparition. Now, as she crossed onto Windward Avenue, the shops and cafes around her turning off their lights, she passed invisibly, an apparition to herself.

She crossed the boardwalk and walked across the beach parking lot, only a few cars here and there in the growing dark. She could hear the ocean waves now, rhythmically rolling against the shore. She removed her light canvas loafers and felt the cool, wet sand on her feet. The vast ocean, home of birth, sprawled and moaned for thousands of miles in front of her. Down the beach, to her left, near the shore, a light flickered. Before, before her encounters in the library, before Scotland with Keats, before Italy with the Shelleys, she would have turned and walked the other way. Now she walked toward it.

A man, he looked middle aged, sat by a small fire of driftwood and trash. His dark hair and beard were disheveled. He wore a black shoreman's cap and an unopened umbrella lay at his side. He held a bottle of vodka on his lap, half-empty, half-full. He offered it to her. Again, before, she wouldn't have taken it. "You're beautiful and wet," he said. And grinned.

She held the bottle, smelled it, then sipped. "So are you," she said.

He laughed a little. "There's a bit of opium in there. Milk of paradise."

She gave the bottle back to him.

"I'm Sam," he said.

"Beatriz," said she.

"Like in Dante?"

"So I'm told," she said.

"A pure heart is best," Sam said. "But if you're going to read him, do it in Italian."

"You read Italian?"

"In my day," he said.

She pointed next to him. "Why don't you use your umbrella?"

He took a swig from the bottle. "You can't wait for your demon lover under an umbrella."

When he offered the bottle again she took it and drank. It took the chill out of her bones. "Are you homeless?" she asked him.

He spread his arms. "How could you call this homeless? Are you homeless?"

"Sometimes," Beatriz said. "Sometimes I am. More timeless than homeless."

"I like that," he said. "May I use it?"

"For what?"

"For a time," he said. "Maybe forever."

She looked out at the ocean, almost black now under a black sky. The wind picked up and she recalled the storm on Shelley's boat. It stirred something in her. Mystery. Somehow comforting mystery.

"Have you heard of the Romantic poets?" she asked him.

He guffawed and drank some more. "Truth is beauty," he said.

"And beauty truth?" Had Keats said that to her? Did he have to?

"Baloney," Sam said.

All right. All right, she thought. Baloney.

"Something has happened inside you nonetheless," Sam said to her. When she didn't respond, couldn't respond, he said, "You are transparent to me."

The rain had stopped. Over the ocean the clouds lifted and on the horizon a star appeared. Sam picked up his umbrella, stood, and leaned on it like cane. "Venus, likely," he said. "You could say I was waiting for her. And maybe for you, too."

He offered her another drink and she took a big one. It transported her. The man in front of her looked suddenly less substantial. She turned away to walk home. She walked, stopped and looked back for Sam. He was gone. But she heard his voice floating over the waves. "I'd stay away from Byron," it said.

VIII

She reached home and drew a hot bath. Her parents owned a hot tub that sat outside their bedroom in the small backyard, but she always felt that using it would be intrusive, for everybody. She examined her legs. Once they got to Italy the girls bathed and groomed each other, though because their dresses covered their armpits and legs, they needn't shave. She'd never gone a month without shaving, but her body hair was sparse and blonde. Yet it seemed that she had more than a week's hair. Nonetheless, that was no way to tell how long she'd been gone. Had she menstruated? She thought not, though she felt it coming on, now, right on schedule, this schedule. The moon, the stars? But she was an urban girl and never paid much attention. On her journeys she'd walked, eaten, dug latrines. Her memory of it, of then, as her memories now, were equally vivid and equally vague. She recalled Keats' soft hands, the warmth of Shelley's chest. The mist, the rain, the warm sun, were the same. There seemed no way of testing one reality against the other. Did she dream two hundred years ago? Did she dream now? Yes, yes, it's all a dream, that cliché explained nothing. If she got pregnant in the 19th century, would she return with the fetus in the 21st? She should carry condoms.

Out of the tub her robe felt soft and warm. She poured some wine. She should read Percy, Mary Shelley, Keats? Not yet. Sam called it purity. As did the woman in Cologne. Was she like Alice? Dorothy? But they both woke up. Besides, she'd only seen the movies. Disney. Then Johnny Depp. She preferred the Disney. Sterling Holloway, the Cheshire Cat. Her own name. Beatriz. She should read Dante, too, someday, but not in Italian.

It felt good to wash and brush out her hair. Her period started. She'd have to give herself a day or two. It felt light.

After a couple of quiet days, sitting, breathing, remembering, she went back to Beyond Baroque. Christina, at her desk, reading something, looked up.

"Thought you might be gone for good," she said. "Coming back or coming to say goodbye?"

"I took a walk in the rain, to the beach."

"Could be dangerous at night, alone."

"I've had some martial arts."

"You and everybody else," said Christina. "Did you run into that homeless drunk who thinks he's Coleridge?"

"He said some unusual things," Beatriz said. "Like stay away from Byron."

"*Childe Harold* or *Don Juan*?" said Christina.

"Maybe he is Coleridge. How would I know?"

"You're the exception that proves the rule," said Christina. "Have you ever thought of going back to school?"

"High school?"

"College. You're smart enough."

"What would I do when they taught the Romantics?"

"Read them?" said Christina.

"My parents taught literature. Wrote some books. I'm staying away from that. Keeping my soul pure."

"And getting cocky about it," Christina said.

Maybe that was true. Her experiences had made her more confident. "I plan to read them. But I want to see this through. Mary should take me to Byron next, no? I want to find out why I should avoid Byron. I'd like to see Keats again."

"There's a poetry reading tonight," said Christina. "And a reception out back in the garden above the library. Marco Delorean."

"Is he important?" said Beatriz.

"I'd say, yes," Christina said.

"A Romantic?"

"A lot's changed in two hundred years."

"Keats would say poetry is eternal," Beatriz said. "Truth and beauty don't change."

"Keats told you that," said Christina.

"In so many words."

"He was a boxer," said Christina.

"He's so little," Beatriz said.

"You don't have to be big to box. He liked to bet on it, too."

"He was tenacious, I guess, now that I think of it."

"It's said he was unkempt."

"I'd say we both were. We walked for miles. Slept outside or in barns." She took Christina 's hand. "I'm going down for a while, but I'll try to come up and catch the reading."

"With your sense of time, good luck," Christina said.

Mary Shelley met her near the library door. "You met Percy," she said to Beatriz.

"And you and Claire Clairton. You must remember," Beatriz said.

"How could I remember you. You didn't exist yet."

"You were a girl when we crossed France. Sixteen."

"There was another girl for a while, besides Claire."

"Me," said Beatriz. "I was nineteen as I am now."

"Are you always nineteen?" said Mary.

"How old are you?" Beatriz said.

"When I'm in this library I can appear as any age I ever was."

"You met Percy at your mother's grave," said Beatriz.

"My birth killed my mother," Mary Shelley said.

"You can't go back?"

"I never knew her."

"Am I re-living your memories?" Beatriz said.

"No. You want an explanation," Mary said. "Nowhere, in no time, are there explanations. Only stories."

"Poems," Beatriz said.

"I was never a poet," said Mary, "but I loved a poet. Married a poet. Maybe the greatest poet."

"Do you see him here?"

Mary Shelley demurred. Then said, "Not really. Not enough. Not actually. We're all ghosts here, monsters, even you. Nothing lasts. If everything lasts forever, then yet nothing lasts. Only our longing." She shimmered in front of Beatriz. For a moment, she was that girl of sixteen.

Beatriz turned. She left the dark library and entered the garden where a crowd had gathered, sipping wine and murmuring. Night had fallen. Small white lights hung from the branches of the surrounding trees. A stage had been set up and a man stood behind a microphone. He was not tall. He had wiry red hair and a red-gray beard. Glasses. He announced "the last poem" he would read, and it was apparent to her that however briefly she'd been below, she yet somehow managed to almost miss the whole reading. The audience quieted.

And the poet began quietly. It almost sounded like he was softly singing. It was about a man and a woman out to dinner. There was tension. They alternately accused, reconciled, accused, reconciled, accused. The man pleaded. He placed his right hand, palm down, in front of her on the table. She picked up her steak knife and drove it through the back of his hand.

The crowd shivered, awed, a few even laughed. The poet thanked them and stepped down. There was loud applause. Christina, who stood to the side of the stage, spotted Beatriz and came to her.

"You made it," said Christina Acevedo.

"Barely," Beatriz said. "Is he always violent?"

"Almost never. That was the shock." She handed Beatriz a copy of Delorean's new book. "Have him sign it," she said.

A small crowd gathered around the poet and she had to wait behind them. Beatriz said, "I feel hypocritical."

"You're not," said Christina. "You might read it."

The little crowd thinned and when Beatriz stepped forward Delorean took the book and opened it. He nodded hello to Christina and to Beatriz he said, "To whom do I have the beautiful pleasure?"

"She said, "Beatriz."

"Like Dante."

"Only with a 'z.'" That much, she'd learned.

"All the better," he said.

Christina introduced her as the new research assistant of the recently discovered library. She and he touched cheeks, and then Christina left the two of them alone.

"The mysterious chamber," the poet said to Beatriz.

"You've heard?" she said.

"Rumors," he said. "Do you write poetry?"

"I don't even read it," she said.

"Well, that doesn't stop a lot of people," and he laughed. "But you have to know the secret handshake."

Beatriz fielded the joke. "Would Shelley know it?"

"See, you know something," Delorean said. "Is Shelley's ghost down there? I'd love to meet him."

By this point, she didn't really know what they were talking about. Did Delorean know something? He couldn't. Was he pulling her leg? Maybe Christina had said something.

"You'd have to get past Mary," Beatriz said.

The poet's eyes widened, then narrowed, then he tilted his left brow toward her. "Can I go down there with you?" he asked.

"Nothing will happen if I bring anyone," said Beatriz.

"The ghosts?"

"Magic or madness," said Beatriz. "But it's only mine. Or for me."

Delorean nodded, not in affirmation, she could see that, but in intrigued skepticism and curiosity. A man intruded, offering Marco Delorean his hand, and Beatriz stepped away.

When she re-entered the library it wasn't the library, but a crowded, candlelit room. Women in gowns, men in waistcoats and high buttoned boots; some wore shoes with large faux buckles and short heels. But for one man who stood off to the side, wearing pantaloons, a short wrap-around jacket and a kind of silk turban that dropped like a scarf over his left shoulder. He didn't wear shoes, but slippers that curled up at the toes. As well as the setting, the atmosphere, her clothes had changed again. She wore a gown like Mary Shelley's that scooped open to her bosom.

A string quartet broke into a waltz and the men and women paired off, but for the oddly dressed man. Without a thought she moved toward him. He spoke, something that wasn't English, but from her sojourn with the Shelleys she recognized Italian.

"English?" she said to him.

He laughed. "Indeed. But I don't waltz. Too much clumsy touching. Are you alone?"

He took her by the elbow and guided her to a tall window that opened to a balcony. He limped slightly. Surrounded by water, a strip of moonlight glistening across.

"Venezia," he said, spreading his arms.

"My home is in Venice too. Another Venice," she said

"In Italy?"

"California," Beatriz said.

"New Spain?" he said. "Far away."

She didn't how to try to explain it, so she said, "You're Lord Byron. Percy Shelley spoke of you."

"Shelley is in Pisa with those Godwin girls. One of them is carrying my child. I'm sailing to Pisa to race boats with Percy. You, headlong, headstrong, young and beautiful. I'd invite you along but I'm traveling with my mistress. Unlike Shelley, I only have one at once. The heart should have only one monopoly."

"At a time," said Beatriz.

"We're alone now or could be." He pointed out to the water. "I love it. I'm an excellent swimmer."

"Unlike Shelley," she said.

Byron laughed. "You are an enchantress, brazen and beguiling. But I don't want to know the depth of your secrets. I prefer magic to knowledge."

"And love," she said, baiting him.

"Is the great magic of the world. Would you like to see me swim?"

"I'd like to swim with you," she said.

"A lady swims?" he said.

"All women in California are good swimmers."

"Mermaids. After I liberate Greece from the Turks I must travel to California. But now, my lady, let's go swim under this moon."

He led her to a street where a one-horse carriage took them to a secluded beach. From the way the gibbous moon sat in the sky, she knew that the shore faced east. There was a small beach house there. In the dressing room a swimsuit hung on a hook. It looked like a large, child's suit, with a flared knee-length skirt and even a blue sailor's scarf attached at the neck. She kept her underpants on where, tucked inside, she kept a condom. Her mother seldom explicitly talked about sex, but it was something Beatriz explicitly remembered: if you're not on birth control, always carry a condom, because he won't. Now, in a premonition, she was satisfied that she did. This wasn't Keats. This was different.

Byron had waited outside wearing something like long underwear that exposed his knees and shins. His legs weren't hairless, his leg hair was light.

"You're legs are smooth," he said to her.

"Yes," she said.

"California," he said. "I like it. What's your name?"

"Beatriz," she said. She pointed at him. "Don't say, 'Like Dante'."

He smiled and laughed softly. He was full-bodied and handsome, dark, wavy hair, a high forehead and strong chin. He pointed toward the sea and a small island that she gauged to be about a quarter mile away, about four hundred meters, a mere eight pool lengths.

"Can you swim there?" he said.

"Yes."

"And back?"

"How else?"

He said, "I won't race ahead."

She said, "Don't worry."

He offered a doubtful grin, and she followed him into the smooth, cool, salty bay. She broke into freestyle next to him. Swimming was easy, like taking a walk if you had a stroke and kick and didn't exhaust yourself gasping for air.

After a little while she flipped into the backstroke, and he laughed in appreciation. He swam powerfully but easily, with the water, not against it. They breast stroked their way to the shore. He took her hand. He said, "Let's rest here in the wavelets, it will keep the sand off."

When she lay down next to him, he faced her. "Like a dance," he said. "You don't need to touch."

"Not while swimming," said Beatriz.

"We're not swimming now," he said, and touched her cheek and kissed her.

She reached under the skirt of her swimsuit and fingered the condom.

PART TWO

IX

Her father kept a mission chair with leather cushions and broad wooden arms. Piles of books surrounded it. She supposed they were related to whatever he was researching, though more often than not his research digressed and branched, not like a tree but a system of streams and tributaries, flowing, sometimes escaping, sometimes flooding, sometimes going dry, sometimes becoming strange books. She knew that he at one time owned thousands of books, novels, religion, history, but when he retired, he threw all of them out; they couldn't be recycled, libraries didn't want them, nor used bookstores, not even thrift stores, an erased labyrinth of who he once had been. Writ on water. He had neither computer nor phone. He now lived, contentedly it seemed, in the ashram of his empty self. He had a bourbon on ice on the arm of his chair. On the floor around him at present, Zen, Proust, Flaubert, Woolf's diaries, Lawrence's *Seven Pillars of Wisdom*. All of that, what would you call it? knowledge? information? Yet he'd never tried to teach her any of it. Then again, she'd never asked.

She sat on a couch to his left, a few feet away. He looked up from "Guermantes Way."

"Do you see yourself as learned?" she asked him.

He smiled, almost laughed, she thought. He was quite white-haired now, both his hair and cropped beard. "Not too long ago people, mostly men then, I suppose, by your age could read and speak Greek and Latin, and other languages, too. I didn't."

"I know that," she said. "I learned it in the library."

"Your job," he said.

She just smiled. She spotted a thick volume on the floor at his feet, the major works of Lord Byron.

"Byron," she said.

"I'm reading *Don Juan*," said her father, Wil. "He can be pretty amusing, among other things."

"I've learned that, too. He was a good swimmer." She paused. "I'm glad you taught me to swim."

Which he'd done, before she was five.

"Me too," he said. "It's fun. To move through the water." He sipped his bourbon. "Would you like some?"

"Okay," she said. She took his glass from him and sipped. It was deeper than the whisky she drank in Scotland. "It's good. You taught a rat to drink bourbon."

"He taught himself," her father said.

A big orange and white cat came into the room. He stopped. Sat and looked at them. Then passed through.

"He's a good mouser," said Wil. "As much as I like rats and mice in general."

"And ants?" she said.

"I admire them, it's true. But you can't live with them in your house. Or eat them, really."

They sat quietly for a while.

"We haven't talked much recently," he finally said.

It was true. In fact she didn't really know why she'd come to him now.

"So we're not talking about the paying job or going back to school," she said to him.

"Somebody has?"

"My supervisor at Beyond Baroque. And Mom."

"Well, your mom and I won't live forever. Teachers don't make much money. We can't promise what will be left for you. Are you picking up any skills in that basement?"

He'd always been frank. Often too frank. Even so, he surprised her. If this was really what they'd meant to talk about, up to now they'd been dancing around it pretty well.

"It's hard to explain," Beatriz said. "I'm learning so much, but I can't say how useful it will be. I think it's helping me find my direction."

He simply nodded.

"When you read a book," she said, "fiction or poetry I mean, do you sometimes fall into its reality?"

He sipped his bourbon. Looked at it.

"It's getting low," she said to him.

"Yes."

"I'll get you more." She took his glass to the kitchen, dumped the melted ice, put in fresh cubes, then poured him a big shot. She brought it to him, and he thanked her.

"I'm a mean reader," he said to her. "I'm really aware or reminding myself that I'm reading. But I can fall in for instants, moments. It doesn't mean it can't happen for longer, depending on who the reader is. Why? Is that happening to you in the library?"

"The Romantic poets," she said.

He pointed to the Byron. "That's really the first I've read."

She wanted an explanation, but how could he understand what she'd fallen into.

"Did you name me after Beatriz in Dante's *Inferno?* she said.

"Beatrice," he said, not using the 'z.' "Your mother named you."

She found her mother sitting at the tall wooden table with its window that faced the yard. She'd taken to feeding the local racoons and a circular, metal tray, rimmed, lay within her vision. She knew the racoons by sight and named them, though she wouldn't feed them cat chow until they looked her in the eyes. "No racoons tonight," she said. "You know they only live for about two years?" She drank tea.

"Do you believe in transmigration?" Beatriz asked.

"Do you mean more than I once did? Racoons, I think, come back as racoons."

"Do poets come back?"

"As poets?" her mother said.

"Maybe we all come back again and again, but we forget," said Beatriz.

"Plato," said Ella, "among others, in the West. But forgetting who we were means forgetting who we are. It's irrelevant. Sartre. Bad faith."

She was easily as well read as her husband. Beatriz looked at her mother's fingers. One simple wedding ring.

"I'm feeling fated right now," Beatriz said. "Fortuned. Maybe, without knowing, I've had good faith."

"You're pretty special, my love," said her mother. "But faith, unfortunately, like karma, is all bad. Necessary and bad. That's some complex, depressing stuff." She sipped her tea.

Beatriz said, "I'm not ready for that yet. But I might be getting ready."

"In the basement library," said her mother. She got up and opened a bottle of wine. The corkscrew had a hinged apparatus that extracted the cork in two, quick silent pulls.

"Trained," said Beatriz.

"Waitressed in my day, as you know."

She had once been nineteen. Lived her life as a smart, beautiful woman.

"Didn't getting educated make you happy?" said Beatriz.

"It got me out of waitressing. But happiness isn't anything that lasts very long."

"Bad happiness?" said Beatriz.

They shared the wine. "You're funny," said her mother. "It made me more confident. It got me a decent job."

"Teaching."

"And writing."

"You never thought of using your beauty to get ahead?"

"Beauty might get you in someone's bed, but it doesn't get you far," her mother, Ella, said. She got up and fetched a tattered paperback from the book shelf. She placed it on the table in front of Beatriz. *Frankenstein*. "You have to start somewhere," she said.

"I'm starting," said Beatriz.

Her father entered the room, carrying his glass of bourbon. He raised it. "Changing the world again?" he said.

Yes," said Beatriz. "Yes, we are."

X

Mary was there. Waiting. She seemed a bit sullen. Beatriz had now read much of the novel. If gripping, she found it sad and horrible. She told that to Mary Shelley.

"I intended it to be neither sad nor horrible," Mary said. "Only frightening. But an author's intention means very little."

"Did Frankenstein intend the monster?"

"Frankenstein was a scientist. A re-animator."

"Did Shelley go mad in Geneva?" Beatriz said. She didn't want to explain that she saw a movie about it. What was a movie to Mary Shelley.

"Hearsay," said Mary Shelley. "A short bout of paranoia. He was a great man. A great poet. A genius. There was no containing his mind. Sometimes it broke out into the world that couldn't comprehend." She paused. "Byron brought a young doctor, a friend, who fell in love with me. Palidori. My step-sister, Claire, was there. And me. It was cold and rainy. We read some German gothic stories that were translated into French. We read aloud. Nothing happened."

"Why didn't you send me there?"

"I've never sent you anywhere," Mary said. "Why are you here now? Anyway, I didn't get the idea for the novel from any of them. Byron suggested that we should all write our own ghost stories, but the weather cleared, and Byron and Shelley went hiking and sailing. I wrote *Frankenstein*. Palidori wrote *The Vampyre*. It was thin, and very short."

"Was Palidori short?" said Beatriz. She was feeling more confidant now.

"Like Keats." Uncontrollably, she smirked. "I didn't consummate Polidori. I wasn't like Percy. Or Claire." She offered Beatriz a penetrating stare. "Or Byron."

Beatriz was taken back, but not troubled. "I met him," she said.

"Undoubtedly," said Mary Shelley.

That night, she looked for Sam on the beach. It wasn't rainy, but yet misty with fog. She spotted the fire and approached. Sam wasn't drinking. He looked cleaner, his eyes more clear, his curly hair brushed.

"I've been waiting for you," he said. He had a small tent behind him. He held a black cat that lounged in his arms. His small fire danced its light upon the rhythm of breaking waves, which seemed to purr more than roar.

"Isn't this illegal?" said Beatriz.

Sam waved his hand at the quiet beach, the shore.

"Wouldn't that necessitate law?" he said. He nodded at his tent. "Would you like to see inside?"

Despite all she'd been through, she had no desire to enter a strange man's tent. "Just take a look," he said. "I won't move."

With all her caution employed, given all her experiences in the library, her curiosity piqued. She moved behind him to the entrance and turned to look back at him. He hadn't budged. So she stooped, lifted the flap, and gazed inside.

Another world.

XI

Below her feet a dark river flowed as quietly as a black moat. In an azure sky sat a pale, waning moon that cast its light into a stand of trees that filled the air with a sweet cedar smell. She touched the riverbank and suddenly floated, rose up. Sam was beside her in the sky. A choir of foreboding voices called in the distance, then one voice, a woman's, stood out like the call of a shore bird, a loon? or no, now a whistling nightingale. It seemed she could see forever, over mountains, cliffs, fertile plains, to a place where the dark river slipped underground. With Sam silently behind her, she flew there, floating through endless exotic canyons, caverns filled with towering stalagmites and swimming stalactites that twisted and turned like dancers, yet not dancers. Now in caverns lit in the same sepia as the library without any explicable source of light, and now through caves of crystalline ice, light danced around them like tiny comets with momentary vaporous tails, a fountain appeared, water cascading, and then an opening to a silent sea, floating above it on a cloud of music, a giant dome. Sam, beside her still, held a cup of warm milk. He sipped. Offered it to her. They both sipped the sweet, honey-dew milk again.

"The milk of paradise," Sam whispered.

They floated toward the dome where the air spilled voices, angry, excited, blissful. Inexplicably they were now inside where the walls spread like swans' wings; there were drinking bars spread against the walls, shadows spread around them like ghosts and here, she thought, it is ghosts who are afraid of men, not women, and women's voices arose; a hymn, the hymn she heard in the ancient convent with Keats; the walls behind the bars were covered with shelves of bottles of myriad colors, each, she knew, promising a separate poison, a different vision, a different journey. Then the shadows fell from the walls and formed a circle around a throne. Sam held her. Gently, he placed her on the throne. "Be our queen," he said. "Count out loud."

She began counting the shadows. In each there was a life, a story, a rhyme, she felt her life a poem, a song, and she found herself yet singing when she stood in front of Christina in her office.

"What are you singing?" Christina said. She wore a dress like a gown that swept down to her feet. Her hair was down on her shoulders, burly, black, and thick.

"I don't know," said Beatriz. She laughed. "What do you do with a drunken sailor?" She laughed again. "I was on the beach. Inside Sam's tent."

"Sam Cooli?"

"Is that his name?"

"Xanadu," said Christina. "That's what he told tourists. Did you eat anything?"

"Warm milk with honey."

"You tripped," Christina said. "You saw things."

"I've taken mushrooms and acid. It wasn't like that," Beatriz said. "This was miraculous."

"When did you do this?"

"Last night, I guess."

"You weren't in the library."

"I walked there," Beatriz said.

Christina turned and fetched her liquor. Poured two glasses of cognac. "Sit down, please." She gently bit her bottom lip. "Sam Cooli died a week ago. The police tried to remove him. He struggled with them, they said. They shot him."

"I just saw him," Beatriz said.

"Show me," said Christina.

Christina drove her small Lexus hybrid down Venice Blvd. and crossed to Windward on Ocean Avenue. She parked and she and Beatriz crossed the parking lot to the beach. Where Sam's tent was once pitched, a few yellow plastic ribbons still rattled in the wind. A vodka fifth, mostly drained, lay among some trash. An old blanket. A dead fire pit. No tent.

"You'd think at least they'd clean up," said Christina.

Beatriz lifted a crime ribbon and let it out, into the ocean breeze pushing shoreward. She'd been here last night. Time and chronology meant nothing.

"You should read "'Kubla Khan'" Christina said. "Xanadu."

"Do you believe I was there?"

"Maybe," said Christina. "If it's immortal. If you are."

"If we all are," Beatriz said. "I need to finish *Frankenstein*."

"Are you coming back to work?"

"Tomorrow," said Beatriz.

"Whenever that is," Christina said.

She found her mother in the living room, reading, listening to Chopin, drinking chamomile tea. Of course, she was reading Coleridge. "Let me read this to you," she said to Beatriz. And she began:

KUBLA KAHN
Samuel Taylor Coleridge

Or a vision in a dream. A fragment

In Xanadu did Kubla Kahn
A stately pleasure dome decree
Where Alph, the sacred river, ran
Through caverns measureless to man
Down to a sunless sea.

Ella read her the complete poem. "Beautiful, no?" said her mother. "He fell asleep on opium and woke up to it, he said."

"I was there, I think," said Beatriz, "I drank the milk."

"Of Paradise? You had a dream?'

"I was awake."

"A drug trip?" her mother said. "Let me get you some tea."

She got up and Beatriz followed her to the kitchen where her mother boiled water in a plug-in kettle, fetched two bags of chamomile, emptied her own cup and got another, then put a tea bag in each cup. The water boiled and she poured it over the tea bags, placed a saucer over each cup to steep the tea. She smiled gently at Beatriz.

"You've been going through something," she said.

"Why were you reading Coleridge?" Beatriz said.

"I don't know," her mother said. "I had a feeling. Frankly, I was thinking about you and I had a feeling."

"You don't think I'm crazy?" She lifted her saucer to check the strength of her tea. It was still a bit pale.

"Chamomile takes a while," said her mother. "Do you want honey . . . or milk?"

Beatriz let that pass. She removed her saucer and squeezed out the bag on her spoon.

"What do you do in the basement library?" Ella asked.

Beatriz was surprised that neither of her parents had asked earlier. Though yet October, it hadn't been that long. "There's a lot of stuff by and about the Romantic poets. I'm trying to straighten it out."

Her mother could have pressed it, but her parents were always careful about her privacy.

Her mother was drinking her tea now, as was she. They sat at the small kitchen table. Afternoon sunlight warmed the room. The tea was hot and calming.

"I feel sorry for the monster," she said.

She could almost read the myriad thoughts racing like . . . like shadows across her mother's expressions, each going unsaid. Her mother was a very implicit being, she realized. She didn't say everything she thought or felt. Years of teaching had taught her to neither pry, presume, or over-teach.

"I need to read more," Beatriz said softly, which meant, I love you, Mom. They were understanding each other. She giggled. Her mother laughed.

When she got to Beyond Baroque Christina emerged from here office. "Marco Delorean was here looking for you," she said.

"The poet."

"Yes."

"Did he say why?" asked Beatriz.

"He said you spoke to him about the library," said Christina.

"I don't remember that," Beatriz said.

"About rumors."

"Rumors?"

"Of ghosts."

"I'm not spreading any rumors," Beatriz said. "I don't even talk to anybody."

"To Sam? said Christina.

"No. Isn't he dead?"

"Would that matter?" said Christina. "Given your adventures."

"Do you think I'm crazy?" asked Beatriz.

"Over imaginative?" Christina said.

"Did Delorean know Sam?"

"Lots of people knew Sam. Or of him."

"I don't think I ever mentioned the library to Sam."

"Your parents?"

"I don't talk to them about it," said Beatriz. "Do you want me to resign?"

Christina looked away from her for a moment. "You're not endangering anyone," she said.

"The Board?" Beatriz said.

"You haven't produced anything," said Christina.

"My non-paying distraction is supposed to produce something?" said Beatriz.

"Lists? Some notes? Anyway, some of them just want to open it up and fill it."

"And pave it?"

"It's not malicious. We're a non-profit. Without more money we could go under. They could use the space." Christina went into the bookstore office and came out with the cognac. "Maybe Delorean could broach the issue with them. Be your ally." She touched her glass to Beatriz'.

"Aren't you my ally?" said Beatriz.

"Not a very powerful one," said Christina. "I'm trying to create a position for you in the bookstore and gallery. A paying position. I mean, what do we make of what's happening around you, and or in you? What do I say?"

Beatriz didn't know. "Maybe this is happening all over the world all the time, throughout time," she said. "Happening to certain people."

"Like psychics or prophets?" said Christina.

"Ordinary people," Beatriz said. "My mother read me 'Kubla Kahn,' yesterday. My father, Byron."

"Maybe she'd heard about Sam," said Christina.

Maybe. Maybe she exuded what was happening to her to those around her. People could *feel* it, without knowing. And Christina could just fire her, that would end it all, but she hadn't done that.

Christina frowned and shook her head, then handed Beatriz a slip of paper. "This is Delorean's cell," she said.

Beatriz added the number to her contacts and headed for the basement library where she showed her battered paperback copy of *Frankenstein* to Mary Shelley.

"That's a reprint of the 1831 edition," Mary Shelley said. "Out there, in your world, when is it now?"

"It's the 21st century."

"Comforting in a way," said Mary.

"I feel sorry for the monster," said Beatriz. "I understand him."

"All monsters are to be pitied. But there are different kinds of monsters, many are human."

"In the preface you said that you just wanted to tell a scary story."

"In *that* preface. The last person to ask about what they wrote is the author. Shelley's poems and the essays he wrote about them are very different," Mary Shelley said. "He wanted to change the world, but poetry doesn't change the world. Look at prayer. Writing is like a prayer."

"You changed the world."

"No, I think not. I was just interested in re-animation and immortality. At the time, I had a lot of creative people around me."

"The monster is a victim," Beatriz said.

"Aren't all monsters victims. All victims monsters. We are all victims. Of God. Of each other. Of ourselves. You need to read Goethe, Shakespeare."

"What is happening here, Mary? Are you my guide?"

"Beatrice is Dante's guide," said Mary Shelley. "So I think you are the guide, taking yourself where you need to go."

But she was ignorant. How could she know where she needed to go? She said that.

Mary said, "That's the best way to do it."

So without saying anything more, Beatriz headed down the Keats aisle, lit in brown light. It widened, then opened to a crowded tavern, no, a pub, raucous and full of drinking men, shouting and reaching out, making bets. There were only a few women there. She felt a strong hand on her arm. A tall, muscular man, features rough, and like his worn clothes looked almost as if they were thrown together. And though he spoke softly, she could hear him through the din.

As the crowd surged toward the back door, he led her gently, deferentially, into the flow of bodies, men stepping aside for them to let them pass. In the yard outside a rope and been laid down in a crude circle under a brooding sky. A man, relatively small, muscular, if not large, stepped into the circle. He was shirtless and wore pants like tights. Another man gave him a shot glass of whisky that he quickly downed. He raised the empty glass and the crowd roared. His name, said her companion, was Tony Magus and he'd never lost a boxing match. He didn't wear boxing gloves.

"You've seen this before?" her companion asked.

She said, no, so he explained. It was a fight. There were really few rules. The fighters could kick, punch, scratch, push. A round ended when one of them went down. If he got up, the fight resumed in thirty seconds. They seldom punched each other's faces because you could easily break your hand on hitting a jaw or skull. It all ended when one of them couldn't get up. The winning betters, in appreciation, gave the winner some of their money.

The crowd began to chant, "Magus! Magus!" as the other fighter entered the ring. It was John Keats.

Then Byron emerged behind him, with a woman, extremely well-jewelled in stones and pearls.

Her companion slowly swung his huge arm and made a space for Beatriz to see. Men stepped aside for the two of them.

"Keats," her new friend said. "And Byron."

"I know them," said Beatriz. "But not the woman."

"The Contessa Teresa Guiccioli," said her friend.

"Isn't Keats ill?" said Beatriz.

Her friend grimaced and tilted his head. It was then that she noticed the scars around his neck and near his ears. "I fought, too," he said to her. "I could beat anyone."

Byron rubbed Keats' shoulders as Keats stared grimly at his opponent. Byron speaking into his ear.

"How can he?" Beatriz said.

And her friend said, "Everyone must fight some time."

Magus stepped forward, as did Keats. Magus lunged for his waist, but Keats sidestepped him. Magus staggered and Keats turned his left shoulder toward him and threw an ineffectual jab. Magus grinned and charged, bringing down both fists on Keats' chest, staggering him. Keats pummeled Magus' chest, again to no effect. Magus tripped him and dropped on top of him, but Keats twisted and pounded on his back. Magus jumped to his feet and so did Keats. They struggled and grappled until Magus pushed away and kicked Keats' groin. Keats went down.

"His asthma," said Beatriz.

And her friend gently touched her shoulders as Keats struggled to his feet. Magus immediately stepped forward and Keats, swinging wildly, landed a hard right to his throat. Magus blinked, fell to his knees, then went totally down on his face. Keats turned away to await the thirty second count as the crowd raged. But before the referee could step in to stop the round, Magus was back on his feet, the crowd roaring. He charged Keats' exposed back. Byron yelled. But too late. Magus' fists came down on the back of Keats' neck, his knee cracked his spine. Keats fell down and out.

Tiny Magus danced, his fists in the air. Around him, men slugged each other. A melee broke out. Beatriz's companion held her with one arm and fended off bodies with the other, knocking men to the ground. Yet fearlessly Beatriz ran into the ring. Keats rolled over and gazed at her. "Fanny," he whispered. He smiled and sat up. When she helped him to his feet, the men nearby cheered him. Tiny Magus touched his chest with his chest, then entered the crowd. Beatriz couldn't see her friend, nor Byron or the Contessa. Keats blinked several times and shook his head. He said, "I should have stayed in med school."

"Where are we?" said Beatriz.

"Brighton," said John Keats. "Brighton Beach. Let's walk to the ocean."

The front of the tavern sat on a boardwalk that followed along the shore. The beach wasn't a beach as she knew them. Instead of sand, the narrow shore consisted of white pebbles. The sun, sailing in the south, glistened off them. Some couples lay together on thick blankets. Behind them, almost like Venice Beach, pubs and shops bristled with noise. The waves gushed on the stones, then crackled when the water receded, the ocean gushing and smacking rhythmically, calmer, yet darker and more threatening than what she knew, the under-roar of the California Pacific.

"Are you hurt?" she asked him.

"No," he said. "There's no shame in losing a fight."

He surprised her, answering for his emotions, his heart, not his wracked body.

"He won unfairly."

"There are no fair fights."

They made their way slowly along the pebbled beach.

"Do you remember me?" she said. "We hiked in Scotland."

"Black flames spreading darkness," he said to her. "That darkness is my light. I remember you. We entered eternity together. For a moment. Maybe a moment of love."

"Beatriz," she said.

"Fanny Beatriz."

"I am not Fanny."

"She is the only one who transcends that."

She is on a beach in England, talking with John Keats about love.

"Can you read Italian?" he asked her.

She simply shook her head.

"You must read Dante," he said to her. "If you are Beatrice. Beatrice is love, suspended by the thread of time between two eternities."

Is that what she had done? Fallen between eternities? She stood before him. "You don't really remember me," she said.

He said, "There's a garden nearby. Let me show you the flowers and the stars."

He took her hand and they left the shore, walking through an alley that opened to a stand of beech trees. The air around them grew silent. "A graveyard for thought. Only poetry can fill it. The poetry of the earth. There's no need for words here. Why are we here in this land between accident and destiny?"

It was often hard to tell if he was speaking to her. Or just shouting his gorgeous madness.

"Yes," she said. "Why now? Here?"

"Because my body is a casket of my soul." He cast his gaze down. "Shelley has asked me to join him in Pisa."

"Will you take Fanny?"

"I'm not going to Pisa. I'll die in Rome. That will be my last gift to Fanny Braun."

She touched his cheek. "You will never die, John Keats."

He looked into her eyes. "My ghost from the future," he said.

He had transformed her. If they had not been lovers then she had yet fallen into his depths. Could she save him?

Once again, almost knowing her thoughts, he said, "You can't stay with me, can't save me. You cannot follow." He kissed her forehead.

She held him. The dusk fell. Above them, a bird burst into song. He didn't need to name it.

XII

She agreed to meet Delorean for coffee at Gjelina on Abbot Kinney.

I was born a block from here," she said to him. "On Electric and Westminster."

"A lot's changed," he said, "but that's tough territory still."

She said, "We moved."

Marco had a latte. She drank red wine. Delorean ordered. She wasn't carded.

"Are you still working down below?" he asked.

"Keats loved boxing," she said.

"Very different back then," said Delorean. He sipped.

"I was shocked," she said.

"Where did you read about that?" he said to her.

She looked him in the eyes. "I didn't," she said.

He let that stand. "When I met you at Beyond Baroque we talked of ghosts," he said.

She nervously gulped her wine. "Did you know Sam Cooli?" she asked.

"Most people in Venice Beach at least knew of him," Delorean said. "It's really impossible to understand, envision a circumstance of him getting shot. By police. He was harmless. He came to Beyond Baroque sometimes for open readings. He read Coleridge. I take it you knew him."

"Did you ever look inside his tent?

"Xanadu?" said Delorean. "No, I never did."

"I think we took a drug," said Beatriz, "and I hallucinated."

Delorean laughed slightly. "Appropriately anyways. Have you run into any Coleridge in your library?"

"Keats said he took a short walk with him that changed his life," Beatriz said.

"I knew that," said Delorean. "In Hampstead. Have you been there?

Now Beatriz laughed. "I've never been anywhere."

Marco Delorean took off his glasses and cleaned them with his handkerchief. He drank some coffee. Put his glasses back on. "You're baiting me," he said. "What aren't you telling me?"

In fact, what could she tell him? Or not tell him? Anything? Everything? None of which could be explained. When she didn't answer him, he said, "Okay, I'd like to meet Shelley." And after another pause. "Like you met him."

Beatriz said, "I walked with him, and Mary and Claire Clairton from Calais to Geneva. We walked across France."

"Well, that's somewhere," Delorean said. "In the 19th century? With their ghosts?"

"Keats says I'm the ghost. From the future. If time exists. But maybe it doesn't. Life is but a day."

"Forever awake," said Marco Delorean.

"In sweet unrest," she said.

"Surely you've read Keats then."

"I plan to," said Beatriz. "Someday."

Delorean leaned forward. "Have you told anyone these things?"

"Only Christina at the bookstore. She fears for my sanity. But even if this is all in my head, it is yet visionary, wouldn't you say?" And what would it matter if Marco Delorean told the world? Who would believe it? Who would listen or care?

Delorean sat back and let out a gentle breath. "So I can't meet Shelley."

"I'm not in control of it. And everything seems to be out of order, or accidental and fateful at the same time. I'm living in fate instead of time. Fate has nothing to do with time."

"Timing," laughed Delorean.

"If that," said Beatriz.

"Like randomly opening a book in different places."

"Does that book have to exist?" she said.

"A simile," he said, "Do you need my help?"

"Are you ever transported when you write?"

"Possessed maybe, at times."

"Like Sam?"

"Not really like that," he said.

She got up.

He took her hand. "Be careful on those sailboats," he said.

But she couldn't. In a moment the hand she held was not Marco Delorean's but Mary Shelley's. Delorean was prescient. They were on a sailboat, a ship. And Shelley inevitably near.

Mary spoke to the rushing wind. "I feel, at times, my marriage has been spent in nightmares and on water. Lakes and streams, rivers, and oceans, with a man who cannot swim, yet he's drawn to them."

They were fleeing Pisa, where Byron and Shelley, both of whom loved to shoot and ride horses, had crossed swords with a local dragoon over their poaching. The dragoon ended up with a pitchfork in his belly. The authorities were unhappy. The dragoon was hospitalized. If he died, somebody was in big trouble. It was Byron's idea to run for it.

Claire was with them. Her daughter, Allegra, a five-year-old sickly child of either Byron's or Shelley's, had been placed in a convent by the two of them, and the troubled Claire convinced to join them in Pisa. Both Byron and Shelley were sleeping with Claire when Allegra, ill and alone, died. All this Mary, now Mary Shelley, told Beatriz.

They were headed for a small fishing village, San Lorenzo, on the Bay of Lerici, joined by another couple, Ed and Jane Williams; Ed was a passionate sailor, Jane sang and played the guitar for and with Percy. Byron and a young, retired naval officer named Trelawny were to join them in San Lorenzo. They were all going to build sailboats.

"This sounds like a mess," Beatriz said.

"I love Shelley. And water," said Mary Shelley. "What are you doing here?"

"That's hard to say," said Beatriz. "You don't remember me?"

"Should I?"

Well, that was hard to say, too. It was, once again, hard to know who was haunting whom. Did ghosts have memories? Did they stalk a time period like holograms? She remembered a friend who read a short book written in the 1920s, about a shipwreck survivor who comes ashore on a populated atoll where none of the inhabitants seemed to see him. From a afar he falls in love with a young woman who wistfully strolls the interior of the island's lagoon, but when he finds the nerve to approach her, she acts as if she can't hear or see him at all. Yet the other people on the atoll interact, talk, eat and drink, dance. Though he finds fruit to eat and water to drink, his hands pass through their food like air. When he goes to look for where they live, he instead finds a building filled with movie projectors and discovers that the people around him are all movies projected into space that run from beginning to end and then begin again; they are projections, immortal images without memories beyond the movie they're in.

"Where did they get the equipment," she said to her friend, "and the power?"

"They were a shipwrecked film crew."

"And who made the movie?"

"The last one standing."

Of course it didn't make sense. It was science fiction. Barely one inference deep. Her father once said to her that some Buddhists often said that reality was a movie and to invest in it would be like mistaking a movie for reality. If the universe was a hologram, what did that change? It's just a metaphor, he said. Metaphors and visions overlapping? But she was here, now, like the sparrow Keats placed in her palm. He could have no memory of his species future extinction. What of Mary Shelley in the library? Or Sam, who would say that time and space are illusory, or at least irrelevant. And where were his memories now? She stood on the deck of a boat with Mary Shelley, who had likely already written *Frankenstein*, unaware of the legacy it would spawn.

When they arrived in San Lorenzo, Mary secured a large house for them all on the lake; four small bedrooms: Mary and Percy shared one, the Williams another, Claire and Beatriz a third, and the fourth had a window overlooking the lake shore, where Shelley wrote or contemplated, though often Mary shared the third room with Beatriz and Claire. The downstairs was small and cramped. Claire was morbidly depressed, Mary worriedly pregnant; she'd lost two already. Almost in sympathy, Percy began sleep walking and ranting, plagued by walking nightmares, he hallucinated that he had a dream where he died and then bloodily murdered each of his housemates, leaving himself alone to grieve.

In one of his sane moments at his window, whimsically gazing at the mountains and the frighteningly blue lake, Beatriz approached him.

He gazed out, his eyes like clouds.

"Me too?" she said to him. "Have you murdered me?"

"Who are you?" Shelley said.

"I sailed with you once," she said.

"You and I?" said Shelley.

"Mary's pregnancy is painful," she said to him.

"It's a ghost child," he said. "It has tried to enter the world, our world, before. But it can't. *Frankenstein* is her only child. No other."

"She needs you," Beatriz said to him.

"In the ocean of my soul, everything is visions. Time and space have vanished. And I must change the world with my words."

Claire, moribund, wasn't speaking, so she approached Williams.

"His boat will arrive," said Ed Williams. "We'll sail. He'll get better."

Why had she been thrown into this tortuous world? Yet maybe she had done some good. Shelley joined them that night for dinner. They drank wine and ate fish soup prepared by Mary. Jane Williams and Shelley sang Irish folk songs and each played the guitar, Jane's eyes flirting with Percy's as they sang.

Afterwards, Shelley spoke of his ideals: universal health care and secular education, the liberation of Ireland and Catholics.

"And women," said Beatriz.

"That day will come," Shelley said. "There will be free love and marriage will be abolished. We will live in a paradise of reason."

"He sounds like my father," Mary whispered to Beatriz. "Only my father doesn't believe those things can happen anymore."

That night, Mary Shelley miscarried. Beatriz held her as she wept.

Days passed. It was hard to know how many. But eventually Mary walked with Beatriz in San Lorenzo, really just a peasant fishing village. They shopped for cheese, fish, chicken, eggs, bread, while Shelley sat by his window, gazing, waiting.

"He will come back to himself," Mary said to Beatriz, "and me. It's impossible to understand the weight of his creativity. He's waiting for his boat. And Byron. He lives in his shadow."

"Byron?"

"Yes. Shelley is deeper, more difficult. But Byron sings to the masses."

In the meantime, up a hill lined with ramshackle apartment buildings, they discovered a small shop, its shelves stacked with wine and beer, gourds, vegetables, and spices. The carcasses of chickens, ducks, and rabbits hung from the rafters. An old woman stood behind a shelved counter that came up to her chest.

Mary said, "Buongiorno," and the woman, her long gray hair piled atop her head, nodded. Mary spoke some Italian, but was obviously a foreigner, in accent and dress. She told the woman they were staying at a house on the lake. The woman, in Italian, said, "I know you. This is a small town."

In that way that you can make out Italian, in bits and pieces, when it spoken to you confidently and plainly, Beatriz could gather snatches.

"I am Giana," said the woman. When Mary and Beatriz said their names, she said, "Ah, Maria and Beatrice, significativi nomi."

"Significant names," Mary said to Beatriz.

Giana picked out some wine and beer, two chickens, potatoes, olive oil, oregano. She fetched a bag of flour and took them to a small kitchen in the back. She pointed to the flour, then to some dough that she'd already made, rolled the dough flat, and then, using a tool like a small rake, cut the dough into thin strips. "Spaghetti," she said.

Mary tried to explain that she and Beatriz couldn't carry it all, even if they could pay for it. Giana put up her palm, left through a back door, and returned with a small burro with cloth bags over his shoulders and back. As she packed the sacks she said, "I know Byron. He likes boats. And women. Will he be coming?"

"Yes," Mary said.

Giana nodded, knowingly, and smiled.

Mary and Beatriz were a big hit when they arrived at the compound, Villa Magni, with their donkey and supplies. After that they traveled to Giana's with their little furry ungulate, now named Fiero, three times a week, though on their way home they sometimes stopped at the pier where the fishermen docked and bought a fresh fish, sea bass or a small tuna, or a bag of anchovies, which they grilled that night. Sometimes Jane pitched in, though she didn't like to cook. Though neither did Beatriz, who marveled that Percy and Edward did nothing domestic at all, though they did on occasion hunt for small game or deer, then they skinned and dressed the meat, which Percy didn't eat. As well, Percy doled out the money for wine and groceries. Percy always complained that he had no money, but he aways seemed to have money. He wasn't a lord, like Byron, but his father and relatives were landowners. He remained desultory until Trelawny and another man, Robert Daniels, showed up with his boat. Shelley was delighted, but for the fact that he'd already named his new sailboat *Ariel*, and Byron, who had supervised the construction, had *Don Juan* plastered in huge script on the topmast. It couldn't be erased, and Percy and Ed had to cut it out and sew in a patch that said *Ariel*.

Now they were set to sail and sail they did. As well, Percy's sensuality re-awakened, and he and Mary were now affectionate constantly. Percy knew that Byron would be on his way, so he determined to send the disconsolate Claire back to Pisa so as not to cross Byron's path there in San Lorenzo. Beatriz found her in their shared room, packing. They'd spent, at times, a good deal of time together, without intimacy or friendship, and the situations were always odd, with Percy dangling his attention between her and Mary. However possible, Claire recused herself. Now, with Percy and Mary a married couple, Shelley gave the impression of a man occupied by monogamy, the excuse for sending Claire back to Pisa. Claire, a beautiful young woman now, wore her sorrow like a veil, and Mary, who proclaimed Claire a peculiar if hidden intellect, took advantage of Percy's temporary resurrection into singular affection and sanity.

"Do you remember crossing France?" Beatriz asked her.

Claire interrupted her folding and looked up, without turning her way. She spoke to the air. "I was a child," she said. "What can you know at fifteen?"

"Do you remember me?"

"In France?"

"And more," said Beatriz.

"That wouldn't make sense," Claire said.

Of course, that was right. Time had passed. Claire was a woman now. And Beatriz lived outside of time, the same age now as then.

"Did you sleep with him?" Claire said.

"No," said Beatriz. "Does it matter?"

"Yes. It's a bond. You think it is. But if anything, you are then more powerless. You don't think you could have less power, but men really have so little room in their hearts."

Beatriz had been sitting on the bed and now stood and stepped toward Claire. "I never consoled you about Allegra."

Claire wept. "I've made mistakes. Look at me. What could I have given her? I was told she didn't ask for me." She looked to Beatriz. "She was Byron's."

"I'm sorry," Beatriz said.

"Yes," said Claire Clairton. "Sorrow. Our lives are ransomed to it." She returned to her packing. "The last time here, Shelley almost died sailing. There was a squall. I'd warned him. He had a girl with him. Mary worried at the shore. I wished them both dead."

In Pisa, she would write to her father in London. If Shelley put enough money in her pocket, he would take her back.

Beatriz. A girl who almost died with Shelley.

At the house, shopping and cooking suddenly fell to Beatriz. She'd never really had that much responsibility before. Giana took it in stride.

"Non parlo Italiano," Beatriz said to her.

"That was Italian," Giana said in English.

"Do you speak English?" said Beatriz.

"No," said Giana. "Seldom anymore."

She showed Beatriz how to make gnocchi from old potatoes, not fresh ones. How to make the dough. How to roll them. It took time. Then how to dice and cook down the tomatoes for sauce. "Oregano," she said.

They now had an intimacy that Beatriz couldn't figure. And Beatriz enjoyed the walk with Fiero through the fishing village. Though Mary didn't like the town or its people, its streets too dusty, its children boisterous and rude. But in time the villagers came to recognize Beatriz and her little burrow, and waved and yelled "Buongiorno!" as they passed by. Giana shared her best wine with her, or coffee.

"Not English," she said to her one day.

"No," said Beatriz. "American."

"Aaah," Giana said to her. "Colombo."

Back at the house, Shelley was insistent that Roberts and Williams help him install more topmasts and sails. He knew Byron would arrive with a big, fast boat and he wanted to be faster.

Trelawny said, "You will never have a faster boat than Byron." Trelawny was pushy and confident. He sported a thin mustache and a patch of beard below the middle of his lower lip. He claimed to have been a naval officer in the Baltic blockade of France and Napoleon, and to have sailed with Nelson at Trafalgar. Though often his stories of heroism, told and retold, didn't match up in the re-telling. Realizing that, she wondered at telling, and re-telling, and what it would mean for her to tell what she'd been going through, and how much of what was happening now was a kind of re-telling. Keats had died. Could her presence here, now, change everything? It was the squall season on these northern lakes. What if he waited? What if he didn't sail?

She found him and Mary having tea in the small kitchen. Shelley was looking vigorous again, his eyes clear, his hair combed and wavy. Mary sat at the corner of the table with him. She looked calm and assured. Trelawny and Roberts had left to fetch Byron. With all the activity and Percy's depression it had been hard to deflect Jane Williams' flirtation; now the playing field had become smaller.

"Have you finished rebuilding your boat?" Beatriz said to Percy.

"Ed and I can finish it," Shelley said.

Beatriz fetched a cup, saucer, and spoon and sat across. "I've heard there can be very sudden, bad storms here in mid-summer."

"You've heard that," he said.

"From the grocer, Giana. She knows the fishermen." She looked at Mary. "He can't swim," she said. "It happened before. He almost drowned."

"But he didn't," Mary said. She touched Shelley's hand. "He's sailing. Not swimming."

"Giana? Do you speak Italian now?" Percy said.

"I'm learning."

"If we capsize in a storm, swimming won't matter."

Did they not remember that she was with him on that near-fatal day? She lay her hand on both of theirs. She looked to Mary Shelley again. How many Mary Shelley's could there be? Was this not the Mary Shelley who guided her to Keats? to Byron? To this. This now. To this time, to prevent a tragedy and in this time, this history, change everything. She whispered inaudibly, "the library," but the Mary in front of her now couldn't remember the future. "I love you both so much," she said. "Wait a month. In August."

"I'll have Williams show you the boat," Shelley said.

And he did. Williams, like Trelawny, was a young, retired military man. He pushed his curly, dark brown hair into a pile on top of his head. She was always surprised that he treated the flirtation between his wife and Percy so casually. He'd become a portrait painter and considered Shelley a great poet and a great man, if not god-like, then at least a nymph of love and of poetry. Shelley could mesmerize.

The boat was on land now, propped up by wooden scaffolding.

"Aren't the masts too tall?" Beatriz said to him. "It doesn't have a keel, or even a deck."

"Speed," Williams said. "We're sailing a lake, not the Atlantic. We'll skim the water like a flying fish."

"Flying fish can swim," Beatriz said.

Then Byron arrived with all his entourage: Trelawny and Roberts in tow, the Countess Teresa Gamba Ghiselli Guiccioli at the bow, servants, dogs, cats, monkeys, parrots. Byron looked like a Turkish prince. His ship, the Bolivar, was gigantic and multi-sailed with two cannons, one port and one starboard; it was more frigate than sailboat. The party followed. Wine flowed. Byron waxed exuberant, Shelley, beneath a half-hearted smile, somber. Trelawny toasted to "the greatest living poets!" Jane Williams, sitting next to Edward, serenaded them, the exquisitely dressed Teresa Guccioli, both haughty and demure, kept Byron near. Mary Shelley massaged Percy's shoulders and sent Beatriz out to fetch more wine.

"Gladly," said the overwhelmed Beatriz.

"But not," said Byron, meeting Beatriz' eyes, "before *Don Juan*," and broke into verse, gesticulating while reciting a speculation on the nature of the soul in a number of forced rhymes, laughing at them, at himself, as he did so. Beatriz nodded to him, then turned to leave.

"A woman who can turn her back on destiny, on several destinies!" pronounced Lord Byron.

"She's not from here," said Mary Shelley, "nor from England. She just appeared among us."

"From the future," said Percy Bysshe.

"From California?" Byron said.

Beatriz turned to him and met his glorious gaze.

Byron lifted his glass to her.

She turned again and left to get the wine. Haltering Fiero, she petted his forehead. She whispered to him, "We have each other." Then they walked through the dusk to Giana's grocery.

Where Giana waited, already having boxed twelve bottles of red wine. She brought the boxes to Beatriz and began slipping the bottles into the sleeves of Fiero's saddle pack.

"Byron is here," she said in English. "I must get ready for him."

"English?" said Beatriz.

"I can speak it. There's no need to show everyone everything."

"You know Byron," Beatriz said.

"I was his lover," said Giana.

But that was impossible. Giana was old before Byron was born.

"I know what you're thinking," Giana said. "It's easy to know what people are thinking. Animals too." She took a carrot from her pocket and gave it to Fiero.

"Can I stop Shelley from sailing?" Beatriz said.

"No one can do that. You're afraid he's going to die."

"More than afraid," Beatriz said.

Giana brought out another bottle of wine and poured for Beatriz and herself into two glass jars. "I sensed that about you," she said. "That you knew things."

"I try to know as little as possible," Beatriz said.

"A good policy." She tapped Beatriz' glass with hers. "I'm a wizard," she said. "Drink up." She did and poured herself more. "I'm about to cast a spell." She wore a full cloak and now wrapped it around herself. "You've slept with him, too," she said. "I know. Not everyone gets to. Don't worry. I'm not jealous."

Beatriz remained silent as Giana raised her cloak over her head. It seemed to float, then fell. Giana had disappeared.

Instantly a gorgeous young woman emerged from the back kitchen. She looked very much like Giana, only many, many years younger, her black hair falling in thick waves upon her shoulders, her eyes amber and sparkling, her skin as white as a sail.

"Giana?" said Beatriz.

"I can appear however I choose," the young woman said. "But this appearance is troublesome and can cause a lot of trouble. Nonetheless, I'm off to see Lord Byron."

"He brought his mistress with him," Beatriz said.

Giana offered a bemused smirk, kissed Beatriz on the cheek and was gone.

What might happen? Beatriz turned to Fiero, but he wasn't there. She wasn't in San Lorenzo anymore, nor Italy at all. She stood in the Beyond Baroque bookstore in front of Christina Acevedo's desk.

"You certainly appear out of nowhere," Christina said.

"Tell me," Beatriz said. "I tried to stop Shelley from sailing on his new boat."

Christina said, "I imagine that didn't go well."

"I don't know what happened," said Beatriz. "I assume he sailed and died."

"Again," said Christina.

For a moment Beatriz thought she looked much like Giana. "Have you been to Italy?" Beatriz said to her.

"No, I haven't. The Board met yesterday."

"Yesterday," said Beatriz. But when was yesterday? And where?

"There are many more businesspeople involved now. They want to raise money," Christina said. "That basement isn't making much money. In fact, none at all."

"They want to get rid of it."

"Destroy it. Bury it. Build on top."

"There's a universe inside," Beatriz said. "Couldn't you tell them that?"

"Tell them what? Do you have anything?" Christina said. "A book? A poem? A word?"

"I'll talk to Marco Delorean," said Beatriz. "I'll take him down."

"To darkness?"

"He's a poet," said Beatriz. "He has that in common." She needed to get away. She headed to the beach. There, between the corners of Windward and Ocean, she saw Sam. He stood before her, amidst the crowds of groups, with his bottle of juiced vodka. He held it out to her. "I miss you," he said.

"Everyone says you're dead. The police shot you."

He offered her his implausible grin. "They tore down my tent. Took all my things."

She took the bottle. Slugged. "Xanadu?"

He didn't answer. He let his head roll slightly. He took back the bottle and drank, then said, "We had a beautiful time, didn't we?"

"They didn't shoot you?"

"I guess they shot somebody."

"Sam," said Beatriz. "Are you Coleridge?"

"You're a beautiful young woman," he said. "But maybe you're nuts. Probably why I like you."

A dead man was telling her she was nuts.

"We didn't go to Xanadu?" she said.

"Where's Xanadu?" said Sam.

"In your tent?"

Sam laughed hard. "You don't have five bucks, do you?"

"They don't pay me at Beyond Baroque," she said. Still, she dug up her wallet and gave him the three ones she had in it. "They're going to destroy the library," she said to him. "All the ghosts of the Romantics."

"That crowd has been dead a long time," said Sam. "They'll go somewhere else, like I just did."

"Do you see them?"

"In my dreams."

"I'm not dreaming."

"Fine, love," said Sam. "Am I alive or dead? We could both be dreaming right now."

She remembered something she'd heard. Where had she heard it? She said, "The universe is a hologram."

"That's a good one," he said. "I like it. God is female. Every black hole an orgasm. Multiple Big Bangs."

"Where are you now, Sam?" she asked him.

"I'm right here."

"Where are you living?"

"In Xanadu?" he laughed. He gave her another slug of laudanum, then kissed her cheek and turned away.

On her way home she texted Delorean. "They are going to bury the library. Sam isn't dead. Meet me?"

He messaged that he couldn't that night. He'd let her know when he was free.

At home, her mother caught her in the yard between the house and her cottage. Her eyes were red from crying.

"Your father has cancer," she said. Her voice trembled. She'd never seen her mother so devastated, so weak. "It's not one they can deal with. It's already traveled."

"Where is he?"

"At UCLA Santa Monica."

"Can I see him?"

"Not now. Maybe in a few days."

"Wine," Beatriz said. She took her mother inside. They sat in the kitchen at the corner of the small table. She opened and poured.

"It comes to this," said her mother. "It must inevitably come to this. Your life disappears and is gone. Unimaginable. You cling to each other, grabbing moments. But you can't stop it."

"They're going to bury the library," said Beatriz.

"I'm sorry," Ella said. "You seem to have given a lot to it."

Beatriz struggled for the words. "I've been totally absorbed by its lives and its times. I go back, trying to preserve and change the past, but I always fail."

Her mother said, "It's my time to be strong."

"I'll be there for you," Beatriz said.

"You have your own life."

"You won't be alone. I'll be there. And there are miracles."

Her mother wept again. "Everything is a miracle."

Beatriz told her about Sam, though she left out the laudanum and Xanadu.

"The homeless man that the police shot."

"I just saw him. He's alive. Mad, but alive."

Her mother sipped her wine. Held back her tears. "I worry for you," she said. She fingered her wedding ring.

"In the library, if I can change nothing, I yet feel indestructible. If only I could stay."

"There?"

"It's hard to describe."

Her mother drank up, bolstering herself. "I have some things to attend to," said Ella. "I'll call you when you can come."

She read Byron's *Don Juan*.

Then, what else was there to do but return to the stacks. She found Mary this time, moving ephemerally amidst her books and letters, and Introductions to Shelley's poems. She appeared as her older self.

"Did you know Coleridge?" she asked her.

"Not well. That older crowd, Coleridge, Wordsworth, even my father, Godwin, grew more conservative as they aged. Coleridge lost cogency to opium. You should read Hazlitt."

"More to read," said Beatriz. "Xanadu."

"He was younger. But when Keats saw him in Hampstead, he said that a two hour walk with Coleridge changed his life."

"Could he be here now?"

"I know nothing about now."

"When I go back, no one remembers me."

"How could they? You weren't alive yet. I don't recall you being there. Back then you are the ghost," said Mary.

"From the future," Beatriz said.

Mary offered a gentle nod.

"You sent me back to prevent their deaths."

"I did not."

"Why not you?"

"Two of me can't exist at the same place at the same time. That's Aristotle."

"I tried and failed."

"Byron will die in Greece," said Mary Shelley.

"I know," said Beatriz. "I read *Don Juan*. I looked it up."

"Will you try to stop him?"

"Yes. My father is dying," Beatriz said.

"I'm sorry," Mary said. "You can't change that either. But you've learned a lot. And so have I. You might change our past in different ways. That's what I have learned. So much for learning."

"You chose me," said Beatriz.

"I did not. Fate chose you."

"They're going to bury this place," Beatriz said.

"There might be other places to go. Besides, it's the future. Do something to change it. Have you read *The Last Man?*"

"I tried. *Don Juan* didn't make much sense."

Mary again offered her gentle nod. "There's a lot more to poetry than sense," she said. "In fact, it's not about sense at all."

"Mary, send me to Byron."

"I'm not the agent in this. I can't."

But something did. In a moment Beatriz was in Geneva, Italy, 1824.

A big house by the sea, Casa Salizzo. A hot day in July. Byron brought eight horses, two dogs, numerous cats, chickens, and geese. His mistress Teresa was there, as was Mary Shelley. Though married now, his wife and daughter, Augusta and Adela, were not with him. Trelawny was to arrive with a wide boat and crew, including a young doctor and Captain Roberts. When Beatriz arrived, Byron had just stormed out of the house, leaving Teresa inside, wailing loudly. She didn't want him to go to Greece and he wouldn't take her with him. He was going to war.

Beatriz had violated an oath to herself and after finishing *Don Juan*, she investigated Lord Byron on Wikipedia. She knew if he left, he wouldn't return.

Again, Mary Shelley hadn't recognized her, but Byron, now standing on the pier, offered her a quizzical lowering of his brow.

"This isn't a tour," he said to her. "It's war. No women."

"We've met," Beatriz said to him. "We swam together. In Venice."

"Swam," he said. "You could keep up with me?"

"Yes."

"You'd think I'd remember that."

"California," she said.

"Where women shave their bodies. And swim."

She kissed him on the lips. She knew that no matter how many women were here, around him, it didn't matter.

He touched her cheek. "I've never known anyone so soft," he said.

She took his hand and walked him down the shore, away from the house, stopping when no one there could see them. On the beach he laid his coat on the sand. There, they lay down on it. It didn't seem presumptive, but comfortably expected, by him and her as well. Utterly, his skin was soft too, but his body as muscular as she remembered. With his wife away, his mistress nearby, his hands, his chest, his heart, his lips, made her feel like the center of all his desire. He knew and pleasured every inch of her, and she made him feel as if she'd known him for a lifetime, or at least two hundred years. This time, they swam afterwards; she taught him the butterfly.

Back on shore, they let the sun dry them. Wistful, he said, "When I return and Greece is free, we must swim again."

"I'm here now because if you leave, you won't return," she said.

"I'm well aware of that possibility," he said.

"It's so certain it's as if it already happened."

"You know the future," he said.

"Keats called me a ghost from the future," she told him.

"You knew Keats," he said.

"I walked with him in Scotland," she said. "And crossed France with the Shelleys and Claire. I might have met Coleridge, too."

"That's a good way of saying it with Coleridge. Did you sleep with them?"

"Only you, my lord," Beatriz said.

"Not even metaphorically?"

"Of course, metaphorically," she said. "I'm like Giana." And this she now believed.

"A witch," he said.

She said, "A woman wizard."

"I'm not afraid to die in battle for a cause," Lord Byron said.

"You won't make it to battle. You'll just get sick and die."

"And you're here now to prevent that inevitable future." She kissed him. His lips were soft and yet receptive. "Here to change history," she whispered.

"Don't go. If you stay, I will stay here too."

"I am Cain," he said. "A dark light. The son of the other God. Do you know Zoroaster?"

"I don't," she said, though later she would read his "Cain" and understand his sympathy for Lucifer, if not his identification.

He began to dress, but she stopped him. Climbed on top of him and placed him inside her. He shuddered and came, violently.

Then she pressed him once more. "Don't go, Lord Byron," she said. She remembered a song her mother loved, and half-sang to him, "Ne me quitte pas. Ne me quitte pas."

He placed his hand softly on her chest. For a moment, his lips quivered. "I must," he said, and turned away.

In the morning, Byron, Trelawny, Roberts, and the doctor with four servants loaded the scow, horses and all, though not the monkey. Beatriz stood at the front window of the house, overlooking the dock, with Teresa, who wept loudly and Mary, who stood there stoically silent. Byron stood at the bow of the boat wearing a combat helmet. He waved once. When they launched, he did not look back.

XIII

At home, in Venice Beach, her father had returned from the hospital. He'd begun chemo and felt and looked lousy. A hospital bed had been brought in, but he sat in his mission chair instead. She went to him alone, without her mother.

He lay back slightly, with the top half of the chair reclined at an angle, a blanket over him. He appeared bare-chested; he notoriously believed that you did not wear clothes to bed, even in a facsimile of a bed. Recovering from surgery, he looked pale. She took his right hand in hers. He offered her a smile.

"I'm sorry," she said.

He said, "You've done something wrong?"

"I wish I knew you better," said Beatriz.

"You mean better than you do right now."

She tried to laugh, but it came out as a kind of grunt.

"It's not an 'if' but a 'when'," he said.

"It's always a when," she said to him.

"That's my girl," her father said. "You know, when somebody asks you a bad question, you always have to say, 'That's a good question,' then answer something else. It's a universal law of conversation."

"Did I ask a bad question?"

"The answer is, my odds aren't good. You should know that I love you and tried to give you as much freedom and security as possible. Your mother and I both have. How's work?"

"It's haunted," she said.

"The library?"

"It's as close as I can get to describing it."

He took a sip of water and then, from another glass, a sip of whisky.

"Whisky?" she said.

"Rye," he said. "What's it going to do, kill me?" He sipped again. "The bottle and glasses are behind the chair."

She retrieved them. She could see he wasn't drunk, but he could always drink a lot.

"Romantic poets," she said.

"There are worse bunches," said her father.

"I've witnessed their deaths in a way."

"Ghosts are no more in control of their lives, or deaths, than we are, I'd guess," he said. "But if I weren't on the verge, you wouldn't have told me."

"Maybe not." She poured them both a shot.

"Our inevitable non-existence is so incomprehensible," he said. "Does your mother know about the library?"

"Obliquely," said Beatriz. "The Board just wants to bury the place and build over it."

"Bury the ghosts?" said her father. "Ironic?"

"Not on their part," though she knew that was his point.

"They've never paid you."

She didn't answer but downed about half of her shot. It was good.

"Poets," said her father.

"Not so much anymore. Just people who want change, to raise money for Beyond Baroque."

"On poetry?" He raised his glass, offered a toast to the air, then drank it down. "Even Cohen had to switch to song writing."

She drank. He poured for them.

"I'll finish chemo, then radiation. I'll feel better for a while, then that's it." He lifted his phone. "Your mother," he said. She nodded. He dialed. Put the phone down. Her mother appeared. Wil poured rye for her. They toasted again.

"It's going to get awful lonely around here," her mother said. Ella had always insisted that Beatriz, and Wil, always refer to her as 'Mom'.

"I'm givin' it all I got Cap'n," said her father.

"He's trying to beat cancer with a bad attitude," said her mother.

Beatriz told her about the Board's plan to bury the library. "I'm going to ask Marco Delorean to try and step in."

"You know him?" said her mother.

"Yes."

"He has a reputation."

"We all do somewhere," said Beatriz.

"My child," said her father.

"He's been a perfect gentleman with me," Beatriz said.

"The most dangerous type," said her father.

"I'm my own person," said Beatriz, "and in my way, recently, I've been around."

"She says the place is haunted," he said to Ella, his life partner. They didn't use the husband-wife stuff around there.

"Sam's not dead, you know," Beatriz said. "I saw him on Ocean and Windward."

"Spoke to him?" her mother asked.

"Yes."

"Have you told anyone?"

"Who would I tell, the police?"

"You see ghosts," her mother said to her.

"It's hard to explain what I've been experiencing there," Beatriz said.

"The Romantic poets," said her father.

"It's more like I'm haunting them."

Things got quiet.

"I read *Don Juan*," Beatriz said.

"Well, that would make anybody see ghosts," said her father. "Though I didn't."

"It almost feels like I read it in my future. Keats called me a ghost from the future."

"Keats called you that," her mother said.

"Mother, you told me that when you read a book, you enter a world. It's like that."

"But what else have you read?"

"*Frankenstein*. I'll read more."

"Are you safe?" said her father.

"I'll be safe," Beatriz said.

Christina was packing up, putting a few books and some Mexican sculpture in a box along with her laptop. She wore jeans, sneakers, and a simple pale blue shirt.

"You're leaving," Beatriz said.

"Things have changed," said Christina.

"Were you fired?"

"I think *you* were fired," said Christina.

"I was never really hired," Beatriz said. "I saw Sam on the corner down by Venice Beach."

Christina looked up. She reached into her box and pulled out a volume of Keats, then handed it to Beatriz. There was a bookmark with a picture of Shelley's marble memorial in Oxford University, the one his sister had made and never got to his grave in Rome. Shelley had been expelled from Oxford for atheism. The bookmark sat between "Ode to a Nightingale" and "Ode to a Grecian Urn." Beatriz opened the book and softly read "Nightingale" aloud. "Was it a vision, or a waking dream?" she ended. "Fled is that music:—Do I wake or sleep?"

Beatriz looked to Christina. "He recited 'When I Have Fears' to me near a stream under a Beech tree. In Scotland."

"Keats did."

"He was only half awake. I think he mistook me for Fanny."

"But you saw Sam here."

Beatriz nodded.

"He pretended to be Coleridge sometimes," Christina said.

"More than pretended, I think," said Beatriz. "Did you pack the cognac yet?" Christina smiled and walked to her desk. She poured two shots of cognac. Beatriz went to her. "My father is very ill," she said.

"I'm sorry," said Christina.

"He might die soon."

"I'm sorry," Christina said again.

They both sipped.

"I'm in touch with Delorean about saving the library."

"What would he be saving?" said Christina. "Your memories. Your imagination?"

"I'll take him down there," Beatriz said.

"I thought you said that Mary Shelley told you no one else," said Christina.

"He's a fellow poet," said Beatriz.

"Do you have your lantern?"

"I never need it. But I'll bring it."

"You can keep that book," Christina said to her.

Beatriz held it to her chest with both hands. "Do you have family?" she said, because with her father dying she suddenly thought of family. Someone there.

"None to speak of."

"What will you do now?"

"There's always something to do," said Christina. "The Last Bookstore downtown is hiring. Keep your keys. Regardless, you won't need them for the library soon." She gave Beatriz a hug. "Stay safe," she said.

Beatriz met Delorean at the same café on Abbot Kinney. He bought her a chardonnay. He got one, too.

"Are you twenty-one?" the waiter asked her

"Would I be here with a teenager?" said Delorean. Everybody in Venice and beyond knew him.

She told him she saw Sam.

"In a dream?" he said.

"On Ocean and Windward."

"I identified him at the morgue," Delorean said.

She collected herself. She started at the beginning and told him everything she could: Mary in the library, Keats, Percy, Claire Clairton, Byron, even Sam. Finally, even Giana. It took a while. They needed another round of wine.

Without expression, he listened. When she was done, he said, "What have you been reading?"

"*Frankenstein* and *Don Juan*.

"That's it?"

"'Nightingale' on several occasions. Keats recited 'When I Have Fears' to me in Scotland."

"Where you've never been," Delorean said.

"Not in this century," she said.

"How do you get there?"

"I go to the library. Sometimes I see Mary. And then I'm there."

Delorean swirled the wine in his glass. The lights in the bar glistened in the swirls. He said, "Who else have you told?"

"Only Christina. But even if I've been gone for days, weeks, she says it's only been a matter of hours."

"That's the least of the mystery," he said. "What did Sam say when you saw him?"

"That he wasn't dead. That I was wonderful but crazy."

Delorean smirked, nodded. They both sipped and sat quietly.

"Marco," she finally said, "the Board wants to bury the library and build on top."

"And Christina?"

"She quit. I guess I was the last straw."

"To say the least," said Delorean.

"But the Board, someone on it, might be swayed by you."

Delorean tilted his brow. He fingered the beard on his chin. Finally, he said, "But what would I be saving?"

"Come down there with me," she said.

"You said no one but you."

"Marco, you're a real poet," said Beatriz.

"Yet you are pure magic."

"Or mad," she said.

"You're not mad," said Delorean. "And I don't want to be the reason this ends for you."

She said, "It will end regardless. How many times can I go back. To what?"

"Would you?" he said.

She hadn't thought that through. But now, thinking about it, there were things, moments, she loved. The library was an astounding portal. What more could she learn there? And bring back? What happened to her was significant. The ghosts of the Romantic poets were somehow there. "Yes," she said. "Come with me." She wept. She didn't want to. But worlds were collapsing around her. "What can I do?"

"Let me think," said Delorean. "I'll call you."

Two days later he called her. They arranged to meet again in a few days, just after dusk, in front of Beyond Baroque. And so they did. They walked through the community garden in the front yard and mounted the old, white marble steps. She put her key in the front door. He touched her hand.

"Are you sure?" he said.

She was sure, as sure as one could ever be about uncertainty. She'd spent the last few days alone in her cottage. She didn't visit her parents but had found a copy of Stanislaw Lem's *Solaris* in the bookstore and slowly read it. It was the most frightening book she'd ever read. Imagine, driven mad and doomed by the fulfillment of your deepest wish.

Inside, she turned on the low, foot-guide emergency lights. She didn't want to light the building and draw anyone's attention. She looked in the bookstore. Christina had, in fact, pulled out. She left Delorean at the bottom of the wide stairway, went up and fetched the kerosene lamp that she'd used briefly in the first few days. Returning, she reminded Marco that no electronic or battery-run devices would work in the basement library. The lantern might not help much either, but with luck they wouldn't need it.

They walked through the main building to the back garden. Outside the library door, Beatriz lit the lantern with a match, then retrieved her key from her pocket and placed it in the lock, turned it, and with her shoulder pushed open the library door. It was dark, but for the light pouring in from the lantern. When she lifted it to peer in, Delorean took her hand. The lantern went out and the place went dark. Delorean brought out his phone, but that failed to light. Its screen went black.

Beatriz tried to light a match, but failed. Now the dark fell ever more heavily.

"Let me try," Delorean said.

Beatriz handed him the matches, but none would light.

"Well that's true," he said. "Weird enough."

In the dark, Beatriz led him, vaguely, to where she remembered the Shelley stacks. They stood there at the head of the dark column of manuscripts and books.

"It should light up now on its own," Beatriz said.

But it didn't light.

Delorean reached out and selected a book. He opened it, but even in the dark he could see that the pages were blank. He reached and opened another, but it, too, was blank.

"Mary," Beatriz called. "Mary Shelley!"

And for a moment the walls and stacks seemed to faintly shimmer. Delorean glanced at his watch, but it had stopped.

"Mary Shelley!" said Beatriz.

The place went dark again.

"It's me!" Beatriz called. "Beatriz!"

But the library remained dark. Beatriz took Marco Delorean's hand and they wandered to the Shelley row, then entered. Still in darkness, Delorean reached for another book. Beatriz grabbed his wrist. "Don't," she said. "I am the blank pages. The writing is in me."

It was too dark to see his expression, yet he did as she said.

"Mary," she said to the silence.

They stood in the dark and quiet. Then, finally, as she resolved to leave, she heard twittering. A bird. The birdsong she'd heard in the convent with Keats. "Listen," she said to the poet, Marco Delorean. "Do you hear it?" It was so very faint.

Delorean said, "No. No, I don't hear anything."

They stood there. The nightingale that only she could hear faded. They stood there in the silence for a long time. They stood there in the dark.

XIV

A girl, a young woman, stands in the dawn on the steps of Beyond Baroque. Men in bright fluorescent vests and yellow plastic construction hats stand around a bulldozer and steam shovel in front of the building on Venice Boulevard. It's November. The air is cold. Steam rises from their white, cardboard coffee cups. Some smoke cigarettes or vape. A few of them are laying orange cones in the street to shut down a lane around the machines. In a little while two dump trucks arrive, one filled with dirt, the other with cement boulders. Their doors display green triangles with blunted corners, beneath them the words Eco-Construction in black letters.

That's when a man with a short beard and a ponytail orders the others to start up. The roar of those giant engines fills the air. A driveway stretches along the main building and this is how they will access the back garden and the underground library. The young woman walks down the steps. She is wearing a full-length beige dress, flats, and a black, cotton shawl, tawny blonde hair falling on her shoulders. She is Beatriz, our heroine. She crosses the front garden on a dirt path and plants herself, standing, in the middle of the driveway, hands at her side, palms facing out. That causes some stirring among the men still on the ground as the bulldozer lurches forward toward the drive. She doesn't move. The foreman breaks from the group and approaches her, stopping about ten feet away and in front of the dozer, which has its shovel raised, obscuring the cockpit and the driver.

"Young lady," the foreman says, pointing at the young woman, "that's where we have to go."

"I'm aware of that," Beatriz says to him. "That's why I'm here."

"Do you work here?" he asks.

"I did," she says. "In the basement library that you want to bury."

"Look," he says. He spread his arms. "This isn't about what we want or don't want. The landowners have paid us to do it. We don't even know what we're covering up."

"Now you know," Beatriz says. "Refuse to do it."

"Then someone else will do it," he says. "Is there something inside that you want?"

"Lives," Beatriz says. "Histories."

"People?"

"Memories."

These workers are part of a private organization. She knows they can't physically touch her. But given what they do, they must have encountered this kind of thing before. He takes out his cell. "I don't want to call the police," he says, but he steps aside and lets the dozer move forward as he dials his phone. The bulldozer lowers its shovel and advances toward her.

She doesn't move. She stands defiantly before the huge metal shovel. Now she can see inside the cab. The driver is the man who protected her against the mob in Brighton, England.

A cold, wet breeze strikes her face. She no longer stands in front of the bulldozer. She is in a stand of trees on the shore of a lake, under a brooding sky. Three men work the sandy shore, poking the ground with the points of their spades. "There were articles here," one says. "Debris." One of the men, the tallest, has deep, tan eyes, a strong chin. He walks with a slight limp. It's Lord Byron. And she recognizes another, Trelawny. She's heard them call the third Hunt. Beatriz feels like a shadow. Mary Shelley's voice whispers behind her, but Beatriz doesn't see her or make out what she's saying.

Byron pokes his shovel into the sand. "Here," he says. "Something hard. A bone."

Trelawny and Hunt move to him and begin digging gently until they discover a body, disfigured by decay. The smell is putrid. They carefully dig around it until it is exposed. It's a man, holding a book as if he died while reading. It's a book of poems by Keats.

"It's Shelley," Byron says.

Beatriz hears a gasp behind her. She knows it's Mary, but she can't see her and knows that she's at home with Jane Williams.

"Williams might be close by," says Hunt.

"It might storm again," says Byron. "Let's deal with this first."

Beatriz backs away as the three of them begin gathering kindling and wood for a pyre. She's barely there. Maybe they don't see her at all.

The kindling gathered and placed, now they stack the wood on top. It's only a few feet from Shelley's corpse, but they transfer him with great difficulty, letting his legs fall from his torso. They place his torso on the pyre, then his legs, then Byron puts the book of poems on his chest. They light the kindling that leaps around him with yellow tongues of flame. It's almost silent but for the waves lapping the shore and the crackling of the flames.

The wind picks up and the wood catches, surrounding Shelley's body in a dance of red and yellow flames. The air above him trembles, tremulous with heat. The lake and sky quiver. Eventually, Beatriz can't tell how long, the flames begin to fall into hot, glowing coals and ash. Trelawny points to something in the coals. "Look," he says, "his heart." It's as if the book of Keats' poems that lay on Shelley's chest had protected it from the fire. With his spade he tries to extricate it from the glowing ash, but the pit is yet hot and he can't maneuver it to lift out the heart.

"Fuck it," says Hunt and thrusts his hands into the ashes to reach the heart, burning his hands as he quickly lifts it and places it on a stone. Then he puts his hands into the lake. "I'll take the heart to Rome and bury it with his ashes next to Keats," he says.

"Give his heart to Mary," says Byron.

"Surely," says Hunt, but Beatriz knows that he kept it for ten years before giving it to her.

They stand quietly as Percy Bysshe Shelley's ashes cool but must retreat to the trees when the storm over the lake overtakes them. The sky darkens and glowers; the air thickens, the lake turns gray and the air, the sky, and the lake become a single torrent. Then it passes and the sky grows calm. The men gather the remaining ashes. They place them in a wooden box with the heart. Byron recovers a few bones.

"It will never storm when I do not think of Shelley," Byron says. "Give his heart to Mary," he tells Hunt.

Beatriz stands in front of the rumbling machine, her eyes now locked on the driver and his on hers. Two squad cars arrive, a man and woman in each. They speak to the foreman, then the women approach Beatriz, one a bit taller than the other.

"Will you come with us?" the tall officer says.

Beatriz doesn't answer.

"You've made your point. But if you resist, we'll have to arrest you," the other officer says.

'My point," Beatriz says. Once again, she locks eyes with the bulldozer driver. She thinks of her mother. Getting arrested would accomplish little.

"Is there something in there we could get for you?" says the tall officer.

"Percy Bysshe Shelley's heart," she says.

"The poet? He's been dead and buried a long time ago," the shorter officer replies.

"Yes," Beatriz says. "Yes."

They take her by her biceps and she lets them lead her away. She directs them to her car. She gets in and drives home.

XV

Marco Delorean never met with the Board. What could he tell them? Within the year he married a young poet and they moved to New York City. Beatriz never went back to Beyond Baroque. She'd played it all wrong. The dozer and steam shovel broke through the ceiling of the library, the trucks filled it with rocks and dirt, then covered it all with cement. The Board announced the construction of a new children's library behind the main building, decorated with gender neutral posters and figurines featuring multiple cultures from every possible race. It had a lot of computer screens and not many books, but for Harry Potter. The old bookstore would remain open, for now. There would be a fundraiser. Beyond Baroque would not close.

Beatriz left messages on Christina's phone, but Christina never returned her calls. When she drove downtown to the Last Bookstore, no one there had any record of her. She visited Venice Beach and sat on the sand where Sam had pitched his tent, but she never saw him again.

At home, she spent time with her father, holding his hand as Ella held the other when he died. For death, there was no recourse, from death, no return. Though she didn't move from the cottage, almost every day she spent time with her mother who was reading Virginia Woolf, and William Butler Yeats. Ella had friends and contemplated travel. On the verge of turning twenty-one Beatriz had not gone back to school but took a job working the front desk at the Museum of Jurassic Technology. Finally, she began reading the Romantics. When she read their biographies, she found that a lot of what she'd experienced was confirmed by their histories. Of course, no mention of her. And she didn't agree with all of it. After all, she knew them. In her backpack she kept a facsimile of the first edition *Frankenstein*.

One spring day, after the rains ended, she drove up the coast and turned onto Topanga Canyon and into Topanga State Park. Being a weekday, there was no one around. Walking in she found a brown lake beneath the spreading oaks, wider and deeper than she remembered, due to a winter of a dozen or more big storms. She sat down on the shore and listened to the jays and sparrows chattering above her. California had no nightingales. The water was still. But suddenly a man stood beside her. A big man, square shouldered, long thick arms ending in ham fists. His clothes, though clean, looked a bit worn and used. She recognized him. The man who helped her on Brighton Beach and who later drove the bulldozer. She unfolded her legs, and though not feeling fear, prepared to jump up and run.

"May I sit with you?" he said, his voice thick and gentle as it had been in Brighton.

"Yes," she said.

He sat down next to her, elbows on his raised knees. A swan circled above them, squawking, then spreading it wings wide, descended onto the lake in front of them, sliding to a stop on the water, not so very far away.

"Gorgeous," he said. "If you saw that a thousand times, it would yet be beautiful."

"Have you?" she said. "Have you seen it a thousand times?"

He smiled softly. "Maybe," he said.

Her experiences in the library made her more brazen with her lived reality. He wasn't like the poets or Mary. Not stuck in time. "We met," she said, "at a boxing match in Brighton Beach. In a saloon. After Keats got knocked down, a brawl broke out. You protected me."

"That would have been a long time ago," he said.

"If you think that time means anything," said Beatriz. "You drove the steam shovel. The others, the poets, I could only visit through the library."

She saw him grow edgy. He clenched and unclenched his massive fists, then clenched them again. If he were who she suspected, he was capable of violence.

"I've followed you," he said. "Then, two hundred years ago, and again now, two hundred years hence. I thought you might help me."

She touched the back of his fist.

"Don't" he said. "I'm a monster, capable of murder. You must know that."

She removed her hand, then reached in her pack and took out her copy of *Frankenstein*.

"I've found that we are all as guilty as we are innocent," she said. "You're not a monster."

He looked at the book. His chest heaved. "Mary Shelley created Frankenstein and Frankenstein created me, dooming me to nameless immortality. I thought if I buried the library, all that had created me would die. And I would die."

She sat by a lake with an impossible being created by a fictional character. If she were imprisoned by fate, he had been imprisoned by creation. She said this to him.

"And so," he said, "Like a wave, I exist for only a moment. I exist forever in each one."

"Nothingness, pushing back," she whispered.

"Yet I remain," he said. "In the midst of woe."

She pointed to the swan now floating in front of them, perfectly still. "Heaven," she said.

He said, "In the white mind of a bird."

He stood. Then she stood. He reached into his jacket and showed her an original edition of *Frankenstein*. "Each part of me was once dead. Apart, each part knew unconscious bliss. Together we suffer hellacious, impossible life." He offered the novel to Beatriz. "Can you let me die?"

"Yes," said Beatriz. She understood now how it could be played out. Her fate. This saga. His fate. Written out on the thread dangling between beauty and horror, between the made up and the real, there exist only moments and a moment can't exist. She took the book from him. She found a flat piece of slate and in some loam nearby began digging. "A grave," she said to him.

"A return," he said.

'I shall bury everywhere you existed, your story, beginning, middle, and end."

She dug a foot or more deep. As he fell to his knees next to her, she placed both her copy and his copy of *Frankenstein* in the grave. He wept. She felt him shuddering at her shoulder. She covered the books with soil. Pressed it down with her palms. His shuddering shook the trees, the ground, the lake. The swan wailed in an abominable squawking. Then, just as suddenly, it ended. She stood and stamped slowly and resolutely on the grave. When she turned to him, he was no longer there. He was gone. The swan, crying, opened its wings and, taking off, flew above her. Its wings filled the sky. ❧

9 781964 295015